SPOOKY STORIES TO TELL IN THE DARK II

GHOSTS, GHOULS, AND OTHER HORRORS

Curated By Chris Ball

Chanthology

No part of this publication may be copied, recorded, transmitted or reproduced in any way without the publisher's express written permission.

All rights reserved
Published by: Chanthology Limited
Communication House, Victoria Avenue, Camberley, Surrey. GU15 3HX. UK.

www.chanthology.com

Paperback Edition: ISBN 978-1-915449-69-6

Hardcover Edition: ISBN 978-1-915449-71-9

Kindle Edition: ISBN 978-1-915449-70-2

CONTENTS

INTRODUCTION

Welcome back, dear reader, to the shadow-laden corridors of "Spooky Stories to Tell in the Dark 2." After the eerie journey we embarked on together through the first volume, your insatiable hunger for the chilling and the macabre has summoned yet another collection from the depths of the unknown. It's with a sense of shared anticipation and a slightly quicker heartbeat that we delve into this next chapter of our exploration into the dark.

Reflecting on our first foray, we danced on the edge of reality and nightmare, with tales that whispered of ancient fears and dark desires. Your courage in facing these tales head-on, your feedback, and the night terrors they inspired, have been the guiding light for this sequel. It's your eagerness to explore the unexplained mysteries and the shadows that lurk just out of sight that have breathed life into this new collection.

"Spooky Stories to Tell in the Dark 2" ventures deeper into the unknown, uncovering tales more chilling and profound. We delve into the spectral presence haunting "An Account of Some Strange Disturbances in Aungier

Street" by J. Sheridan Le Fanu, and sail the cursed seas with "The Ghost Ship" by Richard Barham Middleton. Each story has been meticulously chosen to not only send shivers down your spine but to also challenge your perception of the veil between the living and the dead.

This volume celebrates the power of storytelling, the thrill of the chill that runs down your back, and the primal fear of what lies just beyond the light. These stories connect us not just to the characters within them, but to each other, and to the generations of storytellers and listeners who have sat around firesides, under blankets, or, like us, with a book in hand, eager to be transported to another world.

I invite you, the brave and the curious, to share your experiences and thoughts as you journey through these pages. Connect with fellow readers on our Facebook page at https://www.facebook.com/chanthologylimited and share your eerie experiences on Instagram at https://www.instagram.com/chanthology_/. Let's weave a web of spooky stories enthusiasts, sharing screams, laughs, and maybe even some sleepless nights.

Curating this second volume has been a journey back to those nights spent under the covers with a dim light, where every creak and whisper of the house became part of the story. It has been a reminder of the joy and exhilaration found in the delicious terror of a well-told ghost story. This collection is a tribute to that tradition, an invitation once again to immerse yourself in the thrill of the unknown.

To the tireless spirits who have contributed to this volume, from the authors who have posthumously lent us their nightmares to the living souls who have helped in the compilation and editing process, I extend my deepest gratitude. This collection stands as a testament to the enduring power of storytelling and the unbreakable bond it creates among us.

As you stand on the threshold of "Spooky Stories to Tell in the Dark 2," I challenge you to turn down the lights, cosy into your favourite reading nook, and prepare to be once again mesmerised by the tales that await. Will you dare to confront the horrors that these pages hold? Will you seek out the darkness, knowing the nightmares it may bring?

Welcome back, reader. Your adventure into the heart of darkness continues. May these new tales ignite your imagination, challenge your bravery, and remind you of the delight found in the chill of fear. The shadows await, and the pages turn almost of their own accord. Welcome to "Spooky Stories to Tell in the Dark 2." Let the stories begin.

AN ACCOUNT OF SOME STRANGE DISTURBANCES IN AUNGIER STREET

by J. Sheridan Le Fanu

It is not worth telling this story of mine—at least, not worth writing. Told, indeed, as I have sometimes been called upon to tell it, to a circle of intelligent and eager faces, lighted up by a good after-dinner fire on a winter's evening, with a cold wind rising and wailing outside, and all snug and cosy within, it has gone off—though I say it, who should not—indifferent well. But it is a venture to do as you would have me. Pen, ink, and paper are cold vehicles for the marvellous, and a "reader" is decidedly a more critical animal than a "listener." If, however, you can induce your friends to read it after nightfall and when the fireside talk has run for a while on thrilling tales of shapeless terror; in short, if you will secure me the *mollia tempora fandi*, I will go to my work, and say my say, with better heart. Well, then, these conditions presupposed, I shall waste no more words but tell you simply how it all happened.

My cousin (Tom Ludlow) and I studied medicine together. I think he would have succeeded had he stuck to the profession, but he preferred the Church, poor fellow, and died early, a sacrifice to contagion, contracted in the noble discharge of his duties. For my present purpose, I say enough of his character when I mention that he was of a sedate but frank and cheerful nature, very exact in his observance of truth, and not by any means like myself—of an excitable or nervous temperament.

My Uncle Ludlow—Tom's father—while we were attending lectures, purchased three or four old houses in Aungier Street, one of which was unoccupied. He resided in the country, and Tom proposed that we should take up our abode in the untenanted house, so long as it should continue unlet; a move which would accomplish the double end of settling us nearer alike to our lecture-rooms and to our amusements, and of relieving us from the weekly charge of rent for our lodgings.

Our furniture was very scant—our whole equipage remarkably modest and primitive, and, in short, our arrangements pretty nearly as simple as those of a bivouac. Our new plan was, therefore, executed almost as soon as conceived. The front drawing room was our sitting room. I had the bedroom over it and Tom the back bedroom on the same floor, which nothing could have induced me to occupy.

The house, to begin with, was a very old one. It had been, I believe, newly fronted about fifty years before, but with this exception, it had nothing modern about it. The agent who bought it and looked into the titles for my uncle told me that it was sold, along with much other forfeited property, at Chichester House, I think, in 1702; and had belonged to Sir Thomas Hacket, who was Lord Mayor of Dublin in James II.'s time. How old it was then, I can't say, but, at all events, it had seen years and changes enough to have contracted all that mysterious and saddened air, at once exciting and depressing, which belongs to most old mansions.

There had been very little done in the way of modernising details; and, perhaps, it was better so; for there was something queer and by-gone in the very walls and ceilings—in the shape of doors and windows—in the odd diagonal site of the chimney-pieces—in the beams and ponderous cornices—not to mention the singular solidity of all the woodwork, from the banisters to the window-frames, which hopelessly defied disguise, and would have emphatically proclaimed their antiquity through any conceivable amount of modern finery and varnish.

An effort had, indeed, been made, to the extent of papering the drawing-rooms; but somehow, the paper looked raw and out of keeping; and the old woman, who kept a little dirt-pie of a shop in the lane, and whose daughter—a girl of two and fifty—was our solitary handmaid, coming in at sunrise, and chastely receding again as soon as she had made all ready for tea in our state apartment;—this woman, I say, remembered it, when old Judge Horrocks (who, having earned the reputation of a particularly "hanging judge," ended by hanging himself, as the coroner's jury found, under an impulse of "temporary insanity," with a child's skipping-rope, over the massive old bannisters) resided there, entertaining good company, with fine venison and rare old port. In those halcyon days, the drawing rooms were hung with gilded leather and, I dare say, cut a good figure, for they were really spacious rooms.

The bedrooms were wainscoted, but the front one was not gloomy, and in it, the cosiness of antiquity quite overcame its sombre associations. But the back bedroom, with its two queerly-placed melancholy windows, staring vacantly at the foot of the bed, and with the shadowy recess to be found in most old houses in Dublin, like a large ghostly closet, which, from congeniality of temperament, had amalgamated with the bed chamber, and dissolved the partition. At night-time, this "alcove"—as our "maid" was wont to call it—had, in my eyes, a specially sinister and suggestive character. Tom's distant and solitary candle glimmered vainly into its darkness. There it was, always overlooking him—always itself impenetrable. But this was only part of the effect. The whole room was, I can't tell how, repulsive to me. There was, I suppose, in its proportions and features, a latent discord—a certain mysterious and indescribable relation, which jarred indistinctly upon some secret sense of the fitting and the safe and raised indefinable suspicions and apprehensions of the imagination. On the whole, as I began by saying, nothing could have induced me to pass a night alone in it.

I had never pretended to conceal from poor Tom my superstitious weakness, and he, on the other hand, most unaffectedly ridiculed my tremors. The sceptic was, however, destined to receive a lesson, as you shall hear.

We had not been very long in occupation of our respective dormitories when I began to complain of uneasy nights and disturbed sleep. I was, I suppose, the more impatient under this annoyance, as I was usually a sound sleeper and by no means prone to nightmares. It was now, however, my destiny, instead of enjoying my customary repose every night to "sup full of horrors." After a preliminary course of disagreeable and frightful dreams, my troubles took a definite form, and the same vision, without an appreciable variation in a single detail, visited me at least (on average) every second night of the week.

Now, this dream, nightmare, or infernal illusion—which you please—of which I was the miserable sport, was on this wise:——

I saw or thought I saw, with the most abominable distinctness, although at the time in profound darkness, every article of furniture and accidental arrangement of the chamber in which I lay. This, as you know, is incidental to an ordinary nightmare. Well, while in this clairvoyant condition, which seemed but the lighting up of the theatre in which was to be exhibited the monotonous tableau of horror, which made my nights insupportable, my attention invariably became, I know not why, fixed upon the windows opposite the foot of my bed; and, uniformly with the same effect, a sense of dreadful anticipation always took slow but sure possession of me. I became somehow conscious of a sort of horrid but undefined preparation going forward in some unknown quarter, and by some unknown agency, for my torment; and, after an interval, which always seemed to me of the same length, a picture suddenly flew up to the window, where it remained fixed, as if by an electrical attraction, and my discipline of horror then commenced, to last perhaps for hours. The picture thus mysteriously glued to the window panes, was the portrait of an old man in a crimson flowered silk dressing gown, the folds of which I could now describe, with a countenance embodying a strange mixture of intellect, sensuality, and power, but withal sinister and full of malignant omen. His nose was hooked, like the beak of a vulture; his eyes large, grey, and prominent, and lighted up with a more than mortal cruelty and coldness. These features were surmounted by a crimson velvet cap, the hair that peeped from under which was white with age, while the eyebrows retained their original blackness. Well, I remember every line, hue, and shadow of that stony countenance, and well I may! The gaze of this hellish visage was fixed upon me, and mine returned it with the inexplicable fascination of a nightmare for what appeared to me to be hours of agony. At last——

The cock he crew, away then flew

the fiend who had enslaved me through the awful watches of the night; and, harassed and nervous, I rose to the duties of the day.

I had—I can't say exactly why, but it may have been from the exquisite anguish and profound impressions of unearthly horror, with which this strange phantasmagoria was associated—an insurmountable antipathy to describing the exact nature of my nightly troubles to my friend and comrade. Generally, however, I told him that I was haunted by abominable dreams; and, true to the imputed materialism of medicine, we put our heads together to dispel my horrors, not by exorcism, but by a tonic.

I will do this tonic justice and frankly admit that the accursed portrait began to intermit its visits under its influence. What of that? Was this singular apparition—as full of character as of terror—therefore the creature of my fancy or the invention of my poor stomach? Was it, in short, subjective (to borrow the technical slang of the day) and not the palpable aggression and intrusion of an external agent? That, good friend, as we will both admit, by no means follows. The evil spirit, who enthralled my senses in the shape of that portrait, may have been just as near me, just as energetic, just as malignant, though I saw him not. That means the whole moral code of revealed religion regarding the due keeping of our own bodies, soberness, temperance, etc.? here is an obvious connexion between the material and the invisible; the healthy tone of the system, and its unimpaired energy, may, for aught we can tell, guard us against influences which would otherwise render life itself terrific. The mesmerist and the electro-biologist will fail upon an average with nine patients out of ten—so may the evil spirit. Special conditions of the corporeal system are indispensable to the production of certain spiritual phenomena. The operation succeeds sometimes—sometimes fails—that is all.

I found afterwards that my would-be sceptical companion had his troubles too. But of these, I knew nothing yet. One night, for a wonder, I was sleeping soundly when I was roused by a step on the lobby outside my room, followed by the loud clang of what turned out to be a large brass candlestick, flung with all his force by poor Tom Ludlow over the banisters, and rattling with a rebound down the second flight of stairs; and almost concurrently with this, Tom burst open my door, and bounced into my room backwards, in a state of extraordinary agitation.

I had jumped out of bed and clutched him by the arm before I had any distinct idea of my own whereabouts. There we were—in our shirts—standing before the open door—staring through the great old banister opposite, at the lobby window, through which the sickly light of a clouded moon was gleaming.

"What's the matter, Tom? What's the matter with you? What the devil's the matter with you, Tom?" I demanded, shaking him with nervous impatience.

He took a long breath before he answered me, and then it was not very coherent.

"It's nothing, nothing at all—did I speak?—what did I say?—where's the candle, Richard? It's dark; I—I had a candle!"

"Yes, dark enough," I said, "but what's the matter?—what is it?—why don't you speak, Tom?—have you lost your wits?—what is the matter?"

"The matter?—oh, it is all over. It must have been a dream—nothing at all but a dream—don't you think so? It could not be anything more than a dream."

"Of course," said I, feeling uncommonly nervous, "it was a dream."

"I thought," he said, "there was a man in my room, and—and I jumped out of bed; and—and—where's the candle?"

"In your room, most likely," I said, "shall I go and bring it?"

"No; stay here—don't go; it's no matter—don't, I tell you; it was all a dream. Bolt the door, Dick; I'll stay here with you—I feel nervous. So, Dick, like a good fellow, light your candle and open the window—I am in a shocking state."

I did as he asked me, and robing himself like Granuaile in one of my blankets, he seated himself close beside my bed.

Everybody knows how contagious is fear of all sorts, but more especially that particular kind of fear under which poor Tom was at that moment labouring. I would not have heard, nor I believe he would have recapitulated, just at that moment, for half the world, the details of the hideous vision which had so unmanned him.

"Don't mind telling me anything about your nonsensical dream, Tom," said I, affecting contempt, really in a panic; "let us talk about something else; but it is quite plain that this dirty old house disagrees with us both, and hang me if I stay here any longer, to be pestered with indigestion and—and—bad nights, so we may as well look out for lodgings—don't you think so?—at once."

Tom agreed and, after an interval, said——

"I have been thinking, Richard, that it is a long time since I saw my father, and I have made up my mind to go down tomorrow and return in a day or two, and you can take rooms for us in the meantime."

I fancied that this resolution, obviously the result of the vision which had so profoundly scared him, would probably vanish the next morning with the damps and shadows of night. But I was mistaken. Off went Tom at peep of day to the country, having agreed that so soon as I had secured suitable lodgings, I was to recall him by a letter from his visit to my Uncle Ludlow.

Now, anxious as I was to change my quarters, it so happened, owing to a series of petty procrastinations and accidents, that nearly a week elapsed before my bargain was made and my letter of recall on the wing to Tom; and, in the meantime, a trifling adventure or two had occurred to your humble servant, which, absurd as they now appear, diminished by distance, did certainly at the time serve to whet my appetite for change considerably.

A night or two after the departure of my comrade, I was sitting by my bedroom fire, the door locked, and the ingredients of a tumbler of hot whisky punch upon the crazy spider table; for, as the best mode of keeping the

Black spirits and white,

Blue spirits and grey,

with which I was environed, at bay, I had adopted the practice recommended by the wisdom of my ancestors, and "kept my spirits up by pouring spirits down." I had thrown aside my volume of Anatomy and was treating myself by way of a tonic, preparatory to my punch and bed, to half-a-dozen pages of the Spectator, when I heard a step on the flight of stairs descending from the attics. It was two o'clock, and the streets were as silent as a churchyard—the sounds were, therefore, perfectly distinct. There was a slow, heavy tread, characterised by the emphasis and deliberation of age, descending by the narrow staircase from above; and, what made the sound more singular, it was plain that the feet which produced it was perfectly bare, measuring the descent with something between a pound and a flop, very ugly to hear.

I knew quite well that my attendant had gone away many hours before and that nobody but myself had any business in the house. It was quite plain also that the person who was coming downstairs had no intention whatever of concealing his movements; but, on the contrary, appeared disposed to make even more noise and proceed more deliberately than was at all necessary. When the step reached the foot of the stairs outside my room, it seemed to stop; and I expected every moment to see my door open spontaneously and give admission to the original of my detested portrait. I was, however, relieved in a few seconds by hearing the descent renewed, just in the same manner, upon the staircase leading down to the drawing rooms, and thence, after another pause, down the next flight and so on to the hall, whence I heard no more.

Now, by the time the sound had ceased, I was wound up, as they say, to a very unpleasant pitch of excitement. I listened, but there was not a stir. I screwed up my courage to a decisive experiment—opened my door, and in a stentorian voice, bawled over the banisters, "Who's there?" There was no answer but the ringing of my own voice through the empty old house—no renewal of the movement; nothing, in short, to give my unpleasant sensations a definite direction. There is, I think, something most disagreeably disenchanting in the sound of one's own voice under such circumstances, exerted in solitude and in vain. It redoubled my sense of isolation, and my misgivings increased on perceiving that the door, which I certainly thought I had left open, was closed behind me; in a vague alarm, lest my retreat should be cut off, I got again into my room as quickly as I could, where I remained in a state of imaginary blockade, and very uncomfortable indeed, till morning.

The next night brought no return of my barefooted fellow lodger, but the night following, being in my bed and in the dark—somewhere, I suppose, about the same hour as before, I distinctly heard the old fellow again descending from the garrets.

This time I had had my punch, and the morale of the garrison was consequently excellent. I jumped out of bed, clutched the poker as I passed the expiring fire, and in a moment was upon the lobby. The sound had ceased by this time—the dark and chill were discouraging, and, guess my horror, when I saw, or thought I saw, a black monster, whether, in the shape of a man or a bear, I could not say, standing, with its back to the wall, on the lobby, facing me, with a pair of great greenish eyes shining dimly out. Now, I must be frank and confess that the cupboard which displayed our plates and cups stood just there, though at the moment I did not recollect it. At the same time, I must honestly say that making every allowance for an excited imagination. I never could satisfy myself that I was made the dupe of my own fancy in this matter; for this apparition, after one or two shiftings of shape, as if in the act of incipient transformation, began, as it seemed on second thoughts, to advance upon me in its original form. From an instinct of terror rather than of courage, I hurled the poker, with all my force, at its head; and, to the music of a horrid crash, made my way into my room and double-locked the door. Then, in a minute more, I heard the horrid bare feet walk down the stairs till the sound ceased in the hall, as on the former occasion.

If the apparition of the night before was an ocular delusion of my fancy sporting with the dark outlines of our cupboard, and if its horrid eyes were nothing but a pair of inverted teacups, I had, at all events, the satisfaction of having launched the poker with admirable effect, and in true "fancy" phrase, "knocked its two daylights into one," as the commingled fragments of my tea-service testified. I did my best to gather comfort and courage from this evidence, but it would not do. And then what could I say of those horrid bare feet, and the regular tramp, tramp, tramp, which measured the distance of the entire staircase through the solitude of my haunted dwelling, and at an hour when no good influence was stirring? Confound it!—the whole affair was abominable. I was out of spirits and dreaded the approach of night.

It came, ushered ominously in with a thunderstorm and dull torrents of depressing rain. Earlier than usual, the streets grew silent, and by twelve o'clock nothing but the comfortless pattering of the rain was to be heard.

I made myself as snug as I could. I lit two candles instead of one. I forswore bed and held myself in readiness for a sally, candle in hand; for, coûte qui coûte, I was resolved to see the being, if visible at all, who troubled the nightly stillness of my mansion. I was fidgety and nervous and tried in vain to interest myself in my books. I walked up and down my room, whistling in turn martial and hilarious music and listening ever and anon for the dreaded noise. I sate down and stared at the square label on the solemn and reserved-looking black bottle until "FLANAGAN & CO'S BEST OLD MALT WHISKY" grew into a sort of subdued accompaniment to all the fantastic and horrible speculations which chased one another through my brain.

Silence, meanwhile, grew more silent, and darkness darker. I listened in vain for the rumble of a vehicle or the dull clamour of a distant row. There was nothing but the sound of a rising wind, which had succeeded the thunder storm that had travelled over the Dublin mountains quite out of hearing. In the middle of this great city, I began to feel myself alone with nature and Heaven knows what beside. My courage was ebbing. Punch, however, which makes beasts of so many, made a man of me again—just in time to hear with tolerable nerve and firmness the lumpy, flabby, naked feet deliberately descending the stairs again.

I took a candle, not without a tremour. As I crossed the floor, I tried to extemporise a prayer but stopped short to listen and never finished it. The steps continued. I confess I hesitated for some seconds at the door before I took the heart of grace and opened it. When I peeped out, the lobby was perfectly empty—there was no monster standing on the staircase, and as the detested sound ceased, I was reassured enough to venture forward nearly to the banisters. Horror of horrors! within a stair or two beneath the spot where I stood, the unearthly tread smote the floor. My eye caught something in motion; it was about the size of Goliah's foot—it was grey, heavy, and flapped with a dead weight from one step to another. As I am alive, it was the most monstrous grey rat I have ever beheld or imagined.

Shakespeare says—"Some men there are cannot abide a gaping pig, and some that are mad if they behold a cat." I went well-nigh out of my wits when I beheld this rat; for, laugh at me as you may, it fixed upon me, I thought, a perfectly human expression of malice; and, as it shuffled about and looked up into my face almost from between my feet, I saw, I could swear it—I felt it then, and know it now, the infernal gaze and the accursed countenance of my old friend in the portrait, transfused into the visage of the bloated vermin before me.

I bounced into my room again with a feeling of loathing and horror I cannot describe and locked and bolted my door as if a lion had been at the other side. D—n him or it; curse the portrait and its original! I felt in my soul that the rat—yes, the rat, the RAT I had just seen, was that evil being in masquerade and rambling through the house upon some infernal night lark.

The next morning I was early trudging through the miry streets; and, among other transactions, posted a peremptory note recalling Tom. On my return, however, I found a note from my absent "chum," announcing his intended return the next day. I doubly rejoiced at this because I had succeeded in getting rooms; and because the change of scene and return of my comrade were rendered specially pleasant by the last night's half ridiculous half horrible adventure.

I slept extemporaneously in my new quarters in Digges' Street that night and next morning returned for breakfast to the haunted mansion, where I was certain Tom would call immediately on his arrival.

I was quite right—he came, and almost his first question referred to the primary object of our change of residence.

"Thank God," he said with genuine fervour, on hearing that all was arranged. "On your account, I am delighted. As to myself, I assure you that no earthly consideration could have induced me ever again to pass a night in this disastrous old house."

"Confound the house!" I ejaculated, with a genuine mixture of fear and detestation, "we have not had a pleasant hour since we came to live here," and so I went on and related incidentally my adventure with the plethoric old rat.

"Well, if that were all," said my cousin, affecting to make light of the matter, "I don't think I should have minded it very much."

"Ay, but its eye—its countenance, my dear Tom," urged I; "if you had seen that, you would have felt it might be anything but what it seemed."

"I inclined to think the best conjurer in such a case would be an able-bodied cat," he said with a provoking chuckle.

"But let us hear your own adventure," I said tartly.

At this challenge, he looked uneasily around him. I had poked up a very unpleasant recollection.

"You shall hear it, Dick; I'll tell it to you," he said. "Begad, sir, I should feel quite queer, though, telling it here, though we are too strong a body for ghosts to meddle with just now."

Though he spoke this like a joke, I think it was a serious calculation. Our Hebe was in the corner of the room, packing our cracked delft tea and dinner services in a basket. She soon suspended operations and, with her mouth and eyes wide open, became an absorbed listener. Tom's experiences were told nearly in these words:——

"I saw it three times, Dick—three distinct times; and I am perfectly certain it meant me some infernal harm. I was, I say, in danger—in extreme danger; for, if nothing else had happened, my reason would most certainly have failed me, unless I had escaped so soon. Thank God. I did escape.

"The first night of this hateful disturbance, I was lying in the attitude of sleep in that lumbering old bed. I hate to think of it. I was really wide awake, though I had put out my candle, and was lying as quietly as if I had been asleep; and although accidentally restless, my thoughts were running in a cheerful and agreeable channel.

"I think it must have been two o'clock at least when I thought I heard a sound in that—that odious dark recess at the far end of the bedroom. It was as if someone was drawing a piece of cord slowly along the floor, lifting it up, and dropping it softly down again in coils. I sate up once or twice in my bed but could see nothing, so I concluded it must be mice in the wainscot. I felt no emotion graver than curiosity and, after a few minutes, ceased to observe it.

"While lying in this state, strange to say, without at first a suspicion of anything supernatural, on a sudden I saw an old man, rather stout and square, in a sort of roan-red dressing-gown, and with a black cap on his head, moving stiffly and slowly in a diagonal direction, from the recess, across the floor of the bedroom, passing my bed at the foot, and entering the lumber-closet at the left. He had something under his arm; his head hung a little at one side; and, merciful God! when I saw his face."

Tom stopped for a while and then said——

"That awful countenance, which living or dying I never can forget, disclosed what he was. Without turning to the right or left, he passed beside me and entered the closet by the bed's head.

"While this fearful and indescribable type of death and guilt was passing, I felt that I had no more power to speak or stir than if I had been myself a corpse. For hours after it had disappeared, I was too terrified and weak to move. As soon as daylight came, I took courage and examined the room, and especially the course which the frightful intruder had seemed to take, but there was not a vestige to indicate anybody's having passed there; no sign of any disturbing agency visible among the lumber that strewed the floor of the closet.

"I now began to recover a little. I was fagged and exhausted, and at last, overpowered by a feverish sleep. I came down late; and finding you out of spirits, on account of your dreams about the portrait, whose original I am now certain disclosed himself to me, I did not care to talk about the infernal vision. In fact, I was trying to persuade myself that the whole thing was an illusion, and I did not like to revive in their intensity the hated impressions of the past night—or to risk the constancy of my scepticism, by recounting the tale of my sufferings.

"It required some nerve, I can tell you, to go to my haunted chamber next night and lie down quietly in the same bed," continued Tom. "I did so with a degree of trepidation, which, I am not ashamed to say, a very little matter would have sufficed to stimulate downright panic. This night, however, passed off quietly enough, as also the next, and so too did two or three more. I grew more confident and began to fancy that I believed in the theories of spectral illusions, with which I had at first vainly tried to impose upon my convictions.

"The apparition had been, indeed, altogether anomalous. It had crossed the room without any recognition of my presence: I had not disturbed it, and it had no mission to me. What, then, was the imaginable use of its crossing the room in a visible shape at all? Of course, it might have been in the closet instead of going there, as easily as it introduced itself into the recess without entering the chamber in a shape discernible by the senses. Besides, how the deuce had I seen it? It was a dark night; I had no candle; there was no fire; and yet I saw it as distinctly, in coloring and outline, as ever I beheld human form! A cataleptic dream would explain it all, and I was determined that a dream it should be.

"One of the most remarkable phenomena connected with the practice of mendacity is the vast number of deliberate lies we tell ourselves, whom, of all persons, we can least expect to deceive. In all this, I need hardly tell you, Dick I was simply lying to myself and did not believe one word of the wretched humbug. Yet I went on, as men will do, like persevering charlatans and impostors, who tire people into credulity by the mere force of reiteration, so I hoped to win myself over at last to a comfortable scepticism about the ghost.

"He had not appeared a second time—that certainly was a comfort, and what, after all, did I care for him and his queer old toggery and strange looks? Not a fig! I was nothing the worse for having seen him, and a good story the better. So I tumbled into bed, put out my candle, and, cheered by a loud drunken quarrel in the back lane, went fast asleep.

"From this deep slumber, I awoke with a start. I knew I had had a horrible dream, but what it was I could not remember. My heart was thumping furiously; I felt bewildered and feverish; I sate up in the bed and looked about the room. A broad flood of moonlight came in through the curtainless window; everything was as I had last seen it; and though the domestic squabble in the back lane was, unhappily for me, allayed, I yet could hear a pleasant fellow singing, on his way home, the then popular comic ditty called, 'Murphy Delany.' Taking advantage of this diversion I lay down again, with my face towards the fireplace, and closing my eyes, did my best to think of nothing else but the song, which was every moment growing fainter in the distance:——

"'Twas Murphy Delany, so funny and frisky,

Stept into a shebeen shop to get his skin full;

He reeled out again pretty well lined with whiskey,

As fresh as a shamrock, as blind as a bull.

"The singer, whose condition I dare say resembled that of his hero, was soon too far off to regale my ears anymore, and as his music died away, I myself sank into a doze, neither sound nor refreshing. Somehow the song had got into my head, and I went meandering on through the adventures of my respectable fellow countryman, who, on emerging from the 'shebeen shop,' fell into a river, from which he was fished up to be 'sat upon' by a coroner's jury, who having learned from a 'horse-doctor' that he was 'dead as a door-nail, so there was an end,' returned their verdict accordingly, just as he returned to his senses, when an angry altercation and a pitched battle between the body and the coroner winds up the lay with due spirit and pleasantry.

"Through this ballad, I continued with a weary monotony to plod, down to the very last line, and then da capo, and so on, in my uncomfortable half-sleep, for how long, I can't conjecture. I found myself at last, however, muttering, 'dead as a door-nail, so there was an end'; and something like another voice within me seemed to say, very faintly, but sharply, 'dead! dead! dead! and may the Lord have mercy on your soul!' and instantaneously, I was wide awake and staring right before me from the pillow.

"Now—will you believe it, Dick?—I saw the same accursed figure standing full front and gazing at me with its stony and fiendish countenance, not two yards from the bedside."

Tom stopped here and wiped the perspiration from his face. I felt very queer. The girl was as pale as Tom and, assembled as we were in the very scene of these adventures, we were all, I dare say, equally grateful for the clear daylight and the resuming bustle out of doors.

"For about three seconds only I saw it plainly; then it grew indistinct; but, for a long time, there was something like a column of dark vapour where it had been standing, between me and the wall; and I felt sure that he was still there. After a good while, this appearance went too. I took my clothes downstairs to the hall and dressed there, with the door half open; then went out into the street and walked about the town till morning, when I came back in a miserable state of nervousness and exhaustion. I was such a fool, Dick, as to be ashamed to tell you how I came to be so upset. I thought you would laugh at me, especially as I had always talked philosophy and treated your ghosts with contempt. I concluded you would give me no quarter and so kept my tale of horror to myself.

"Now, Dick, you will hardly believe me when I assure you that for many nights after this last experience, I did not go to my room at all. I used to sit up for a while in the drawing room after you had gone up to your bed and then steal down softly to the hall door, let myself out, and sit in the 'Robin Hood' tavern until the last guest went off, and then I got through the night like a sentry, pacing the streets till morning.

"For more than a week, I never slept in bed. I sometimes had a snooze on a form in the 'Robin Hood,' and sometimes a nap in a chair during the day, but with regular sleep, I had absolutely none.

"I was quite resolved that we should get into another house, but I could not bring myself to tell you the reason, and I somehow put it off from day to day, although my life was, during every hour of this procrastination, rendered as miserable as that of a felon with the constables on his track. I was growing absolutely ill from this wretched mode of life.

"One afternoon, I determined to enjoy an hour's sleep upon your bed. I hated mine; so that I had never, except in a stealthy visit every day to unmake it, lest Martha should discover the secret of my nightly absence, entered the ill-omened chamber.

"As ill luck would have it, you had locked your bedroom and taken away the key. I went into my own to unsettle the bedclothes, as usual, and give the bed the appearance of having been slept in. Now, a variety of circumstances concurred to bring about the dreadful scene through which I was that night to pass. In the first place, I was literally overpowered with fatigue and longing for sleep; in the next place, the effect of this extreme exhaustion upon my nerves resembled that of a narcotic and rendered me less susceptible than, perhaps, I should in any other condition have been, of the exciting fears which had become habitual to me. Then again, a little bit of the window was open. A pleasant freshness pervaded the room, and, to crown all, the cheerful sun of the day was making the room quite pleasant. What was to prevent my enjoying an hour's nap here? The whole air was resonant with the cheerful hum of life, and the broad matter-of-fact light of day filled every corner of the room.

"I yielded—stifling my qualms—to the almost overpowering temptation, and merely throwing off my coat and loosening my cravat, I lay down, limiting myself to half-an-hour's doze in the unwonted enjoyment of a feather bed, a coverlet, and a bolster.

"It was horribly insidious, and the demon, no doubt, marked my infatuated preparations. Dolt that I was, I fancied, with mind and body worn out for want of sleep, and an arrear of a full week's rest to my credit, that such measure as half an hour's sleep in such a situation was possible. My sleep was death-like, long, and dreamless.

"Without a start or fearful sensation of any kind, I waked gently but completely. It was, as you have good reason to remember, long past midnight—I believe, about two o'clock. When sleep has been deep and long enough to satisfy nature thoroughly, one often wakens in this way, suddenly, tranquilly, and completely.

"There was a figure seated in that lumbering, old sofa chair near the fireplace. Its back was rather towards me, but I could not be mistaken; it turned slowly round, and, merciful heavens! there was the stony face, with its infernal lineaments of malignity and despair, gloating on me. There was now no doubt as to its consciousness of my presence and the hellish malice with which it was animated, for it arose and drew close to the bedside. There was a rope about its neck, and the other end, coiled up, it held stiffly in its hand.

"My good angel nerved me for this horrible crisis. I remained for some seconds, transfixed by the gaze of this tremendous phantom. He came close to the bed and appeared on the point of mounting upon it. The next instant, I was upon the floor at the far side, and in a moment more was, I don't know how upon the lobby.

"But the spell was not yet broken; the valley of the shadow of death was not yet traversed. The abhorred phantom was before me there; it was standing near the banisters, stooping a little, and with one end of the rope around its own neck, was poising a noose at the other, as if to throw over mine; and, while engaged in this baleful pantomime, it wore a smile so sensual, so unspeakably dreadful, that my senses were nearly overpowered. I saw and remembered nothing more until I found myself in your room.

"I had a wonderful escape, Dick—there is no disputing that—an escape for which, while I live, I shall bless the mercy of heaven. No one can conceive or imagine what it is for flesh and blood to stand in the presence of such a thing but one who has had the terrific experience. Dick, Dick, a shadow has passed over me—a chill has crossed my blood and marrow, and I will never be the same again—never, Dick—never!"

Our handmaid, a mature girl of two-and-fifty, as I have said, stayed her hand as Tom's story proceeded, and by little and little drew near to us, with open mouth, and her brows contracted over her little, beady black eyes, till stealing a glance over her shoulder now and then, she established herself close behind us. During the relation, she had made various earnest comments, with an undertone; but these and her ejaculations, for the sake of brevity and simplicity, I have omitted in my narration.

"It's often I heard tell of it," she now said, "but I never believed it rightly till now—though, indeed, why should not I? Does not my mother, down there in the lane, know quare stories, God bless us, beyant telling about it? But you ought not to have slept in the back bedroom. She was loath to let me be going in and out of that room even in the day time, let alone for any Christian to spend the night in it; for sure she says it was his own bedroom."

"Whose own bedroom?" we asked, in a breath.

"Why, his—the ould Judge's—Judge Horrock's, to be sure, God rest his sowl"; and she looked fearfully round.

"Amen!" I muttered. "But did he die there?"

"Die there! No, not quite there," she said. "Shure, was not it over the banisters he hung himself, the ould sinner, God be merciful to us all? and was not it in the alcove they found the handles of the skipping-rope cut off and the knife where he was settling the cord, God bless us, to hang himself with? It was his housekeeper's daughter who owned the rope, my mother often told me, and the child never throve after and used to be starting up out of her sleep, and screeching in the night time, wid dhrames and frights that cum an her, and they said how it was the speerit of the ould Judge that was tormentin' her; and she used to be roaring and yelling out to hould back the big ould fellow with the crooked neck; and then she'd screech 'Oh, the master! the master! he's stampin' at me, and beckoning to me! Mother, darling, don't let me go!' And so the poor crathure died at last, and the docthers said it was wather on the brain, for it was all they could say."

"How long ago was all this?" I asked.

"Oh, then, how would I know?" she answered. "But it must be a wondherful long time ago, for the housekeeper was an ould woman, with a pipe in her mouth, and not a tooth left, and better nor eighty years ould when my mother was first married; and they said she was a rale buxom, fine-dressed woman when the ould Judge come to his end; an', indeed, my mother's not far from eighty years ould herself this day; and what made it worse for the unnatural ould villain, God rest his soul, to frighten the little girl out of the world the way he did, was what was mostly thought and believed by every one. My mother says how the poor little crathure was his own child; for he was by all accounts an ould villain every way, an' the hangin'est judge that ever was known in Ireland's ground."

"From what you said about the danger of sleeping in that bedroom," said I, "I suppose there were stories about the ghost having appeared there to others."

"Well, there was things said—quare things, surely," she answered, as it seemed, with some reluctance. "And why would not there? Sure was it not up in that same room he slept for more than twenty years? and was it not in the alcove he got the rope ready that done his own business at last, the way he done many a betther man's in his lifetime? —and was not the body lying in the same bed after death, and put in the coffin there, too, and carried out to his grave from it in Pether's churchyard, after the coroner was done? But there was quare stories—my mother has them all— about how one Nicholas Spaight got into trouble on the head of it."

"And what did they say of this Nicholas Spaight?" I asked.

"Oh, for that matther, it's soon told," she answered.

And she certainly did relate a very strange story, which so piqued my curiosity, that I took occasion to visit the ancient lady, her mother, from whom I learned many very curious particulars. Indeed, I am tempted to tell the tale, but my fingers are weary, and I must defer it. But if you wish to hear it another time, I shall do my best.

When we had heard the strange tale I have not told you, we put one or two further questions to her about the alleged spectral visitations to which the house had, ever since the death of the wicked old Judge, been subjected.

"No one ever had luck in it," she told us. "There were always cross accidents, sudden deaths, and short times in it. The first that tuck, it was a family—I forget their name— but at any rate there was two young ladies and their papa. He was about sixty and a stout healthy gentleman as you'd wish to see at that age. Well, he slept in that unlucky back bedroom, and God between us an' harm! sure enough he was found dead one morning, half out of the bed, with his head as black as a sloe, and swelled like a puddin', hanging down near the floor. It was a fit, they said. He was as dead as a mackerel, and so he could not say what it was, but the ould people was all sure that it was nothing at all but the ould Judge, God bless us! that frightened him out of his senses and his life together.

"Sometime after, there was a rich old maiden lady who took the house. I don't know which room she slept in, but she lived alone; and at any rate, one morning, the servants going down early to their work found her sitting on the passage stairs, shivering and talkin' to herself, quite mad; and never a word more could any of them or her friends get from her ever afterwards but, 'Don't ask me to go, for I promised to wait for him.' They never made out from her who it was she meant by him, but of course, those that knew all about the ould house were at no loss for the meaning of all that happened to her.

"Then afterwards, when the house was let out in lodgings, there was Micky Byrne that took the same room, with his wife and three little children; and sure I heard Mrs Byrne myself telling how the children used to be lifted up in the bed at night, she could not see by what mains; and how they were starting and screeching every hour, just all as one as the housekeeper's little girl that died, till at last one night poor Micky had a dhrop in him, the way he used now and again; and what do you think in the middle of the night he thought he heard a noise on the stairs, and being in liquor, nothing less id do him but out he must go himself to see what was wrong. Well, after that, all she ever heard of him was himself sayin', 'Oh, God!' and a tumble that shook the very house; and there, sure enough, he was lying on the lower stairs, under the lobby, with his neck smashed double undher him, where he was flung over the banisters."

Then the handmaiden added——

"I'll go down to the lane, and send up Joe Gavvey to pack up the rest of the taythings, and bring all the things across to your new lodgings."

And so we all sallied out together, each of us breathing more freely, I have no doubt, as we crossed that ill-omened threshold for the last time.

Now, I may add thus much, in compliance with the immemorial usage of the realm of fiction, which sees the hero not only through his adventures but fairly out of the world. You must have perceived that what the flesh, blood, and bone hero of romance proper is to the regular compounder of fiction, this old house of brick, wood, and mortar is to the humble recorder of this true tale. I, therefore, relate, as in duty bound, the catastrophe which ultimately befell it, which was simply this—that about two years subsequently to my story it was taken by a quack doctor, who called himself Baron Duhlstoerf and filled the parlour windows with bottles of indescribable horrors preserved in brandy, and the newspapers with the usual grandiloquent and mendacious advertisements. This gentleman, among his virtues, did not reckon sobriety, and one night, being overcome with much wine, he set fire to his bed curtains, partially burned himself, and totally consumed the house. It was afterwards rebuilt, and for a time an undertaker established himself on the premises.

I have now told you my own and Tom's adventures, together with some valuable collateral particulars, and having acquitted myself of my engagement, I wish you a very good night and pleasant dreams.

HAUNTED

by J. Sheridan Le Fanu

A few years ago, one of those great national conventions which draw together all ages and conditions of the sovereign people of America was held in Charleston, South Carolina. Colonel Demarion, one of the State Representatives, had attended that great national convention; and, after an exciting week, was returning home, having a long and difficult journey before him.

A pair of magnificent horses, attached to a light buggy, flew merrily enough over a rough country for a while; but toward evening, stormy weather reduced the roads to a dangerous condition and compelled the Colonel to relinquish his purpose of reaching home that night, and to stop at a small wayside tavern, whose interior, illuminated by blazing wood-fires, spread a glowing halo among the dripping trees as he approached it, and gave promise of warmth and shelter at least.

Drawing up to this modest dwelling, Colonel Demarion saw through its uncurtained windows that there was no lack of company within. Beneath the trees, too, an entanglement of rustic vehicles, giving forth red gleams from every dripping angle, told him that beasts as well as men were cared for. At the open door appeared the form of a man, who, at the sound of wheels, but not seeing in the outside darkness whom he addressed, called out, "'Tain't no earthly use a-stoppin' here."

Caring more for his chattels than for himself, the Colonel paid no further regard to this address than to call loudly for the landlord.

At the tone of authority, the man in outline more civilly announced himself to be the host; yet so far from inviting the traveller to alight, insisted that the house was "as full as it could pack;" but that there was a place a little farther down the road where the gentleman would be certain to find excellent accommodation.

"What stables have you here?" demanded the traveller, giving no more heed to this than to the former announcement, but bidding his servant to alight, and preparing to do so himself.

"Stables!" repeated the baffled host, shading his eyes so as to scrutinize the newcomer, "stables, Cap'n?"

"Yes, stables. I want you to take care of my horses; I can take care of myself. Some shelter for cattle you must have by the look of these traps," pointing to the wagons. "I don't want my horses to be kept standing out in this storm, you know."

"No, Major. Why no, cert'n'y; Marion's ain't over a mile, and——"

"Conf—!" muttered the Colonel, "but it's over the river, which I don't intend to ford to-night under any consideration."

So saying, the Colonel leaped to the ground, directing his servant to cover the horses and then get out his valise; while the host, thus defeated, assumed the best grace he could to say that he would see what could be done "for the horses."

"I am a soldier, my man," added the Colonel in a milder tone as he stamped his cold feet on the porch and shook off the rain from his travelling gear; "I am used to rough fare and a hard couch: all we want is shelter. A corner of the floor will suffice for me and my rug; a private room I can dispense with at such times as these."

The landlord seemed no less relieved at this assurance than mollified by the explanation of a traveller whom he now saw was of a very different stamp from those who usually frequented the tavern. "For the matter of stables, his were newly put up, and first-rate," he said, and "cert'n'y the Gen'ral was welcome to a seat by the fire while 'twas a-storming so fierce."

Colonel Demarion gave orders to his servant regarding the horses while the landlord, kicking at what seemed to be a bundle of sacking down behind the door, shouted—"Jo! Ho, Jo! Wake up, you sleepy-headed nigger! Be alive, boy, and show this gentleman's horses to the stables." Upon repetition of which charges, a tall, gaunt, dusky figure lifted itself from out of the dark corner and grew taller and more gaunt as it stretched itself into waking with a grin which was the most visible part of it, by reason of two long rows of ivory gleaming in the red glare. The hard words had fallen as harmless on Jo's ear-drum as the kicks upon his impassive frame. To do Jo's master justice, the kicks were not vicious kicks, and the rough language was but an intimation that dispatch was needed. Very much of the spaniel's nature had Jo, and as he rolled along the passage to fetch a lantern, his mouth expanded into a still broader grin at the honor of attending so stately a gentleman. Quick, like his master, too, was Jo to discriminate between "real gentlefolks" and the "white trash" whose rough-coated, rope-harnessed mules were the general occupants of his stables.

"Splendid pair, sir," said the now conciliating landlord. "Shove some o' them mules out into the shed, Jo (which your horses 'll feel more to hum in my new stalls, Gen'ral)."

Again cautioning his man Plato not to leave them one moment, Colonel Demarion turned to enter the house.

"You'll find a rough crowd in here, sir," said the host, as he paused on the threshold, "but a good fire, anyhow. 'Tain't many of these loafers as understand this convention business—I presume, Gen'ral, you've attended the convention—they all on 'em thinks they does, tho'. Fact most on 'em thinks they'd orter be on the committee theirselves. Good many on 'em is from Char'ston to-day, but is in the same fix as yerself, Gen'ral—can't get across the river to-night."

"I see, I see," cried the statesman, with a gesture toward the sitting room. "Now what have you got in your larder, Mr Landlord? and send some supper out to my servant; he must make a bed of the carriage-mats to-night."

The landlord introduced his guest into a room filled chiefly with that shiftless and noxious element of Southern society known as "mean whites." Pipes and drinks, and exciting arguments, engaged these people as they stood or sat in groups. The host addressed those who were gathered around the log fire, and they opened a way for the new-comer, some few, with republican freedom, inviting him to be seated, the rest giving one furtive glance, and then, in antipathy born of envy, skulking away.

The furniture of this comfortless apartment consisted of sloppy, much-jagged deal tables, dirty, whittled benches, and a few uncouth chairs. The walls were dirty with accumulated tobacco stains, and so moist and filthy was the floor that the sound only of scraping seats and heavy footsteps told that it was of boards and not bare earth.

Seated with his back toward the majority of the crowd and shielded by his newspaper, Colonel Demarion sat awhile unobserved; but was presently recognized by a man from his own immediate neighborhood when the information was quickly whispered about that no less a person than their distinguished Congressman was among them.

This piece of news speedily found its way to the ears of the landlord, to whom Colonel Demarion was known by name only, and forthwith he reappeared to overwhelm the representative of his State with apologies for the uncourteous reception which had been given him and to express his now very sincere regrets that the house offered no suitable accommodation for the gentleman. Satisfied as to the safety of his chattels, the Colonel generously dismissed the idea of having anything either to resent or to forgive and assured the worthy host that he would accept no exclusive indulgences.

In spite of which, the landlord bustled about to bring in a separate table, on which he spread a clean coarse cloth and a savory supper of broiled ham, hot corncakes, and coffee; every few minutes stopping to renew his apologies, and even appearing to grow confidentially communicative regarding his domestic economies; until the hungry traveller cut him short with "Don't say another word about it, my friend; you have not a spare sleeping-room, and that is enough. Find me a corner—a clean corner"—looking round upon the most unclean corners of that room— "perhaps up-stairs somewhere, and——"

"Ah! upsta'rs, Gen'ral. Now, that's jest what I had in my mind to ax you. Fact is ther' is a spar' room upsta'rs, as comfortable a room as the best of folks can wish; but——"

"But it's crammed with sleeping folks, so there's an end of it," cried the senator, thoroughly bored.

"No, sir, ain't no person in it; and ther' ain't no person likely to be in it 'cept 'tis yerself, Colonel Demarion. Leastways——"

After a good deal of hesitation and embarrassment, the host, in mysterious whispers, imparted the startling fact that this most desirable sleeping room was haunted; that the injury he had sustained in consequence had compelled him to fasten it up altogether; that he had come to be very suspicious of admitting strangers, and had limited his custom of late to what the bar could supply, keeping the matter hushed up in the hope that it might be the sooner forgotten by the neighbors but that in the case of Colonel Demarion he had now made bold to mention it; "as I can't but think, sir," he urged, "you'd find it prefer'ble to sleepin' on the floor or sittin' up all night along ov these loafers. Fer if 'tis any deceivin' trick got up in the house, maybe they won't try it on, sir, to a gentleman of your reputation."

Colonel Demarion became interested in the landlord's confidences but could only gather in further explained that for some time past all travellers who had occupied that room had "made off in the middle of the night, never showin' their faces at the inn again;" that on endeavoring to arrest one or more in their nocturnal flight, they—all more or less terrified—had insisted on escaping without a moment's delay, assigning no other reason than that they had seen a ghost. "Not that folks seem to get much harm by it, Colonel—not by the way they makes off without paying a cent of money!"

Great indeed was the satisfaction evinced by the victim of unpaid bills on the Colonel's declaring that the haunted chamber was the very room for him. "If to be turned out of my bed at midnight is all I have to fear, we will see who comes off master in my case. So, Mr Landlord, let the chamber be got ready directly, and have a good fire built there at once."

The exultant host hurried away to confide the great news to Jo and with him to make the necessary preparations. "Come what will, Jo, Colonel Demarion ain't the man to make off without paying down good money for his accommodations."

In reasonable time, Colonel Demarion was beckoned out of the public room, and conducted upstairs by the landlord, who, after receiving a cheerful "good-night," paused on the landing to hear his guest bolt and bar the door within, and then push a piece of furniture against it. "Ah," murmured the host, as a sort of misgiving came over him, "if a apparishum has a mind to come thar, 'tain't all the bolts and bars in South Carolina as 'll kip'en away."

But the Colonel's precaution of securing his door, as also that of placing his revolvers in readiness, had not the slightest reference to the reputed ghost. Spiritual disturbances of such kind he feared not. Spirits tangible were already producing ominous demonstrations in the rooms below, nor was it possible to conjecture what troubles these might evolve. Glad enough to escape from the noisy company, he took a survey of his evil-reputed chamber. The only light was that of the roaring, crackling, blazing wood fire, and no other was needed. And what storm-benighted traveller, when fierce winds and rains are lashing around his lodging, can withstand the cheering influences of a glorious log fire? Especially if, as in that wooden tenement, that fire be of abundant pine knots. It rivals the glare of gas and the glow of a furnace; it charms away the mustiness and fustiness of years and causes all that is dull and dead around to laugh and dance in its bright light.

By the illumination of just such a fire, Colonel Demarion observed that the apartment offered nothing worthier of remark than that the furniture was superior to anything that might be expected in a small wayside tavern. In truth, the landlord had expended a considerable sum in fitting up this, his finest chamber, and had, therefore, sufficient reason to bemoan its unprofitableness.

Having satisfied himself as to his apparent security, the senator thought no more of spirits palpable or impalpable; but to the far graver issues of the convention, his thoughts reverted. It was yet early; he lighted a cigar and, in full appreciation of his retirement, took out his notebook and plunged into the affairs of state. Now and then, he was recalled to the circumstances of his situation by the swaggering tread of unsteady feet about the house or when the boisterous shouts below raged above the outside storm, but even then, he only glanced up from his papers to congratulate himself upon his agreeable seclusion.

Thus he sat for above an hour, then he heaped fresh logs upon the hearth, looked again to his revolvers, and retired to rest.

The house clock was striking twelve as the Colonel awoke. He awoke suddenly from a sound sleep, flashing, as it were, into full consciousness, his mind and memory clear, all his faculties invigorated, his ideas undisturbed, but with a perfect conviction that he was not alone.

He lifted his head. A man was standing a few feet from the bed and between it and the fire, which was still burning, and burning brightly enough to display every object in the room and to define the outline of the intruder clearly. His dress also and his features were plainly distinguishable: the dress was a travelling costume, in a fashion somewhat out of date; the features wore a mournful and distressed expression—the eyes were fixed upon the Colonel. The right arm hung down, and the hand, partially concealed, might, for aught the Colonel knew, be grasping one of his own revolvers; the left arm was folded against the waist. The man seemed about to advance still closer to the bed and returned the occupant's gaze with a fixed stare.

"Stand, or I'll fire!" cried the Colonel, taking in all this at a glance, and starting up in his bed, revolver in hand.

The man remained still.

"What is your business here?" demanded the statesman, thinking he was addressing one of the roughs from below.

The man was silent.

"Leave this room, if you value your life," shouted the indignant soldier, pointing his revolver.

The man was motionless.

"Retire! or by heaven I'll send a bullet through you!"

But the man moved not an inch.

The Colonel fired. The bullet lodged in the breast of the stranger, but he started not. The soldier leapt to the floor and fired again. The shot entered the heart, pierced the body, and lodged in the wall beyond and the Colonel beheld the hole where the bullet had entered, and the firelight glimmering through it. And yet the intruder stirred not. Astounded, the Colonel dropped his revolver and stood face to face before the unmoved man.

"Colonel Demarion," spake the deep, solemn voice of the perforated stranger, "in vain you shoot me—I am dead already."

The soldier, with all his bravery, gasped, spellbound. The firelight gleamed through the hole in the body, and the eyes of the shooter were riveted there.

"Fear nothing," spake the mournful presence; "I seek but to divulge my wrongs. Until my death shall be avenged my unquiet spirit lingers here. Listen."

Speechless, motionless was the statesman; and the mournful apparition thus slowly and distinctly continued:

"Four years ago I travelled with one I trusted. We lodged here. That night my comrade murdered me. He plunged a dagger into my heart while I slept. He covered the wound with a plaster. He feigned to mourn my death. He told the people here I had died of heart complaint; that I had long been ailing. I had gold and treasures. With my treasure secreted beneath his garments he paraded mock grief at my grave. Then he departed. In distant parts he sought to forget his crime; but his stolen gold brought him only the curse of an evil conscience. Rest and peace are not for him. He now prepares to leave his native land forever. Under an assumed name that man is this night in Charleston. In a few hours he will sail for Europe. Colonel Demarion, you must prevent it. Justice and humanity demand that a murderer roam not at large, nor squander more of the wealth that is by right my children's."

The spirit paused. To the extraordinary revelation, the Colonel had listened in rapt astonishment. He gazed at the presence, at the firelight glimmering through it—through the very place where a human heart would be—and he felt that he was indeed in the presence of a supernatural being. He thought of the landlord's story, but while earnestly desiring to sift the truth of the mystery, words refused to come to his aid.

"Do you hesitate?" said the mournful spirit. "Will you also flee, when my orphan children cry for retribution?" Seeming to anticipate the will of the Colonel, "I await your promise, senator," he said. "There is no time to lose."

With a mighty effort, the South Carolinians said, "I promise. What would you have me do?"

In the same terse, solemn manner, the ghostly visitor gave the real and assumed names of the murderer, described his person and dress at the present time and described a certain curious ring he was then wearing, together with other distinguishing characteristics: all being carefully noted down by Colonel Demarion, who, by degrees, recovered his self-possession, and pledged himself to use every endeavor to bring the murderer to justice.

Then, with a portentous wave of the hand, "It is well," said the apparition. "Not until the spirit of my murderer shall be separated from the mortal clay can my spirit rest in peace." And vanished.

Half-past six in the morning was the appointed time for the steamer to leave Charleston, and the Colonel lost not a moment in preparing to depart. As he hurried down the stairs, he encountered the landlord, who—his eyes rolling in terror—made an attempt to speak. Unheeding, except to demand his carriage, the Colonel pushed past him and effected a quick escape toward the back premises, shouting lustily for "Jo" and "Plato," and for his carriage to be got ready immediately. A few minutes more, and the bewildered host was recalled to the terrible truth by the noise of the carriage dashing through the yard and away down the road, and it was some miles nearer Charleston before the unfortunate man ceased to peer after it in the darkness—as if by so doing he could recover damages—and bemoan to Jo the utter ruin of his house and hopes.

Thirty miles of hard driving had to be accomplished in little more than five hours. No great achievement under favorable circumstances, but the horses were only half refreshed from their yesterday's journey, and though the storm was over, the roads were in a worse condition than ever.

Colonel Demarion resolved to be true to his promise, and fired by a curiosity to investigate the extraordinary communication which had been revealed to him, urged on his horses, and reached the wharf at Charleston just as the steamer was being loosed from her moorings.

He hailed her. "Stop her! Business with the captain! Stop her!"

Her machinery was already in motion; her iron lungs were puffing forth dense clouds of smoke and steam; and as the Colonel shouted—the crowd around, from sheer delight in shouting, echoing his "Stop her! stop her!"—the voices on land were confounded with the voices of the sailors, the rattling of chains, and the haulings of ropes.

Among the passengers standing to wave farewells to their friends on the wharf were some who recognized Colonel Demarion and drew the captain's attention toward him and as he continued vehemently to gesticulate, that officer, from his post of observation, demanded the nature of the business which should require the ship's detention. Already the steamer was clear of the wharf. In another minute, she might be beyond the reach of the voice; therefore, failing by gestures and entreaties to convince the captain of the importance of his errand, Colonel Demarion, in desperation, cried at the top of his voice, "A murderer on board! For God's sake, stop!" He wished to have made this startling declaration in private, but not a moment was to be lost, and the excitement around him was intense.

In the midst of the confusion, another cry of "Man overboard!" might have been heard in a distant part of the ship had not the attention of the crowd been fastened on the Colonel. Such a cry was, however, uttered, offering a still more urgent motive for stopping, and the steamer being again made fast, Colonel Demarion was received on board.

"Let not a soul leave the vessel!" was his first and prompt suggestion, and with the order being issued, he drew the captain aside and concisely explained his grave commission. The captain thereupon conducted him to his private room and summoned the steward, before whom the details were given, and the description of the murderer was read over. The steward, after considering attentively, seemed inclined to associate the description with that of a passenger whose remarkably dejected appearance had already attracted his observation. In such a grave business it was, however, necessary to proceed with the utmost caution, and the "passenger-book" was produced. Upon reference to its pages, the three gentlemen were totally dismayed by the discovery that the name of this same dejected individual was that under which, according to the apparition, the murderer had engaged his passage.

"I am here to charge that man with murder," said Colonel Demarion. "He must be arrested."

Horrified as the captain was at this astounding declaration, yet, on account of the singular and unusual mode by which the Colonel had become possessed of the facts, and the impossibility of proving the charge, he hesitated in consenting to the arrest of a passenger. The steward proposed that they should repair the saloons and deck and, while conversing with one or another of the passengers, mention—as it were casually—in the hearing of the suspected party his own proper name and observe the effect produced on him. To this, they agreed and, without loss of time, joined the passengers, assigning some feasible cause for a short delay of the ship.

The saloon was nearly empty, and while the steward went below, the other two repaired to the deck, where they observed a crowd gathered seaward, apparently watching something over the ship's side.

During the few minutes which had detained the captain in this necessarily hurried business, a boat had been lowered, and some sailors had put off in her to rescue the person who was supposed to have fallen overboard, and it was only now, on joining the crowd, that the captain learned the particulars of the accident. "Who was it?" "What was he like?" they exclaimed simultaneously. That a man had fallen overboard was all that could be ascertained. Someone had seen him run across the deck, looking wildly about him. A splash in the water had soon afterwards attracted attention to the spot, and a body had since been seen struggling on the surface. The waves were rough after the storm and thick with seaweed, and the sailors had as yet missed the body. The two gentlemen took their post among the watchers and kept their eyes intently upon the waves and upon the sailors battling against them. Ere a long, they see the body rise again to the surface. Floated on a powerful wave, they can, for a few moments, breathlessly scrutinize it. The color of the dress is observed. A face of agony upturned displays a peculiar contour of forehead; the hair, the beard; and now he struggles—an arm is thrown up, and a remarkable ring catches the Colonel's eye. "Great heavens! The whole description tallies!" The sailors pull hard for the spot. The next stroke and they will rescue——

A monster shark is quicker than they. The sea is tinged with blood. The man is no more!

Shocked and silent, Colonel Demarion and the captain quit the deck and resummoned the steward, who had, but without success, visited the berths and various parts of the ship for the individual in question. Every hole and corner was now, by the captain's order, carefully searched but in vain, and as no further information concerning the missing party could be obtained, and the steward persisted in his statement regarding his general appearance, they proceeded to examine his effects. In these, he was identified beyond doubt. Papers and relics proved not only his guilt but his remorse, remorse which, as the apparition had said, permitted him no peace in his wanderings.

Those startling words, "A murderer on board!" had doubtless struck fresh terror to his heart and, unable to face the accusation, he had thus terminated his wretched existence.

Colonel Demarion revisited the little tavern and on several occasions, occupied the haunted chamber, but never again had he the honor of receiving a midnight commission from a ghostly visitor, and never again had the landlord bemoan the flight of a non-paying customer.

THE HAUNTED AND THE HAUNTERS

by Edward Bulwer Lytton

A friend of mine, who is a man of letters and a philosopher, said to me one day, as if between jest and earnest—"Fancy! since we last met, I have discovered a haunted house in the midst of London."

"Really haunted?—and by what?—ghosts?"

"Well, I can't answer these questions—all I know is this—six weeks ago I and my wife were in search of a furnished apartment. Passing a quiet street, we saw on the window of one of the houses a bill, 'Apartments Furnished.' The situation suited us: we entered the house— liked the rooms—engaged them by the week—and left them the third day. No power on earth could have reconciled my wife to stay longer, and I don't wonder at it."

"What did you see?"

"Excuse me—I have no desire to be ridiculed as a superstitious dreamer—nor, on the other hand, could I ask you to accept on my affirmation what you would hold to be incredible without the evidence of your own senses. Let me only say this, it was not so much what we saw or heard (in which you might fairly suppose that we were the dupes of our own excited fancy, or the victims of imposture in others) that drove us away, as it was an undefinable terror which seized both of us whenever we passed by the door of a certain unfurnished room, in which we neither saw nor heard anything. And the strangest marvel of all was, that for once in my life I agreed with my wife—silly woman though she be—and allowed, after the third night, that it was impossible to stay a fourth in that house. Accordingly, on the fourth morning, I summoned the woman who kept the house and attended on us, and told her that the rooms did not quite suit us, and we would not stay out our week. She said, dryly: 'I know why; you have stayed longer than any other lodger; few ever stayed a second night; none before you, a third. But I take it they have been very kind to you.'

"'They—who?' I asked, affecting a smile.

"'Why, they who haunt the house, whoever they are. I don't mind them; I remember them many years ago when I lived in this house, not as a servant, but I know they will be the death of me someday. I don't care—I'm old and must die soon, anyhow, and then I shall be with them and in this house still.' The woman spoke with so dreary a calmness that really it was a sort of awe that prevented my conversing with her farther I paid for my week, and too happy were I and my wife to get off so cheaply."

"You excite my curiosity," said I; "nothing I should like better than to sleep in a haunted house. Pray, give me the address of the one which you left so ignominiously."

My friend gave me the address, and when we parted, I walked straight towards the house thus indicated.

It is situated on the north side of Oxford Street in a dull but respectable thoroughfare. I found the house shut up—no bill at the window and no response to my knock. As I was turning away, a beer boy collecting pewter pots at the neighbouring areas said to me, "Do you want anyone in that house, sir?"

"Yes, I heard it was to let."

"Let!—why the woman who kept it is dead—has been dead these three weeks, and no one can be found to stay there, though Mr J—— offered ever so much. He offered mother, who chars for him, £1 a week just to open and shut the windows, and she would not."

"Would not!—and why?"

"The house is haunted, and the old woman who kept it was found dead in her bed with her eyes wide open. They say the devil strangled her."

"Pooh!—you speak of Mr J——. Is he the owner of the house?"

"Yes."

"Where does he live?"

"In G—— Street, No. ——."

"What is he?—in any business?"

"No, sir—nothing particular; a single gentleman."

I gave the pot-boy the gratuity earned by his liberal information and proceeded to Mr J——, in G——Street, which was close by the street that boasted the haunted house. I was lucky enough to find Mr J—— at home—an elderly man with an intelligent countenance and prepossessing manners.

I communicated my name and my business frankly. I said I heard the house was considered to be haunted—that I had a strong desire to examine a house with so equivocal a reputation—that I should be greatly obliged if he would allow me to hire it, though only for a night. I was willing to pay for that privilege, whatever he might be inclined to ask. "Sir," said Mr J——, with great courtesy, "the house is at your service for as short or as long a time as you please. Rent is out of the question—the obligation will be on my side should you be able to discover the cause of the strange phenomena which at present deprive it of all value. I cannot let it, for I cannot even get a servant to keep it in order or answer the door. Unluckily the house is haunted, if I may use that expression, not only by night, but by day, though at night the disturbances are of a more unpleasant and sometimes of a more alarming character.

"The poor old woman who died in it three weeks ago was a pauper whom I took out of a workhouse, for in her childhood she had been known to some of my family, and had once been in such good circumstances that she had rented that house of my uncle. She was a woman of superior education and a strong mind and was the only person I could ever induce to remain in the house. Indeed, since her death, which was sudden, and the coroner's inquest, which gave it a notoriety in the neighbourhood, I have so despaired of finding any person to take charge of it, much more a tenant, that I would willingly let it rent-free for a year to anyone who would pay its rates and taxes."

"How long is it since the house acquired this sinister character?"

"That I can scarcely tell you, but very many years since. The old woman I spoke of said it was haunted when she rented it between thirty and forty years ago. The fact is that my life has been spent in the East Indies and in the civil service of the Company. I returned to England last year on inheriting the fortune of an uncle, amongst whose possessions was the house in question. I found it shut up and uninhabited. I was told that it was haunted and that no one would inhabit it. I smiled at what seemed to me so idle a story. I spent some money on repainting and roofing it— added to its old-fashioned furniture a few modern articles —advertised it, and obtained a lodger for a year. He was a colonel retired on half-pay. He came in with his family, a son and a daughter, and four or five servants: they all left the house the next day, and although they deponed that they had all seen something different, that something was equally terrible to all. I really could not in conscience sue, or even blame, the colonel for breach of the agreement.

"Then I put in the old woman I have spoken of, and she was empowered to let the house in apartments. I never had one lodger who stayed more than three days. I do not tell you their stories—to no two lodgers have there been exactly the same phenomena repeated. It is better that you should judge for yourself than enter the house with an imagination influenced by previous narratives; only be prepared to see and to hear something or other, and take whatever precautions you yourself please."

"Have you never had a curiosity yourself to pass a night in that house?"

"Yes. I passed not a night but three hours in broad daylight alone in that house. My curiosity is not satisfied, but it is quenched. I have no desire to renew the experiment. You cannot complain, you see, sir, that I am not sufficiently candid, and unless your interest be exceedingly eager and your nerves unusually strong, I honestly add that I advise you not to pass a night in that house."

"My interest is exceedingly keen," said I, "and though only a coward will boast of his nerves in situations wholly unfamiliar to him, yet my nerves have been seasoned in such variety of danger that I have the right to rely on them —even in a haunted house."

Mr J—— said very little more; he took the keys of the house out of his bureau, gave them to me,—and thanking him cordially for his frankness and his urbane concession to my wish, I carried off my prize.

Impatient for the experiment, as soon as I reached home, I summoned my confidential servant—a young man of gay spirits, fearless temper, and as free from superstitious prejudice as anyone I could think of.

"F——," said I, "you remember in Germany how disappointed we were at not finding a ghost in that old castle, which was said to be haunted by a headless apparition? Well, I have heard of a house in London which, I have reason to hope, is decidedly haunted. I mean to sleep there tonight. From what I hear, there is no doubt that something will allow itself to be seen or to be heard— something, perhaps, excessively horrible. Do you think, if I take you with me, I may rely on your presence of mind, whatever may happen?"

"Oh, sir! pray trust me," answered F——, grinning with delight.

"Very well—then here are the keys of the house—this is the address. Go now—select for me any bedroom you please, and since the house has not been inhabited for weeks, make up a good fire—air the bed well—see, of course, that there are candles as well as fuel. Take with you my revolver and my dagger—so much for my weapons—arm yourself equally well; and if we are not a match for a dozen ghosts, we shall be but a sorry couple of Englishmen."

I was engaged for the rest of the day on business so urgent that I had not leisure to think much on the nocturnal adventure to which I had plighted my honour. I dined alone and very late, and while dining, I read as is my habit. The volume I selected was one of Macaulay's Essays. I thought to myself that I would take the book with me; there was so much healthfulness in style, and practical life in the subjects, that it would serve as an antidote against the influences of superstitious fancy.

Accordingly, at about half-past nine, I put the book into my pocket and strolled leisurely towards the haunted house. I took with me a favourite dog—an exceedingly sharp, bold, and vigilant bull-terrier—a dog fond of prowling about strange ghostly corners and passages at night in search of rats—a dog of dogs for a ghost.

It was a summer night, but chilly, the sky somewhat gloomy and overcast. Still, there was a moon—faint and sickly, but still a moon—and if the clouds permitted, after midnight, it would be brighter.

I reached the house, knocked, and my servant opened with a cheerful smile.

"All right, sir, and very comfortable."

"Oh!" said I, rather disappointed; "have you not seen nor heard anything remarkable?"

"Well, sir, I must own I have heard something queer."

"What?—what?"

"The sound of feet pattering behind me; and once or twice small noises like whispers close at my ear—nothing more."

"You are not at all frightened?"

"I! not a bit of it, sir", and the man's bold look reassured me on one point—viz. that, happen what might, he would not desert me.

We were in the hall, the street door closed, and my attention was now drawn to my dog. He had at first ran in eagerly enough but had sneaked back to the door and was scratching and whining to get out. After patting him on the head and encouraging him gently, the dog seemed to reconcile himself to the situation and followed me and F —— through the house, but keeping close at my heels instead of hurrying inquisitively in advance, which was his usual and normal habit in all strange places. We first visited the subterranean apartments, the kitchen and other offices, and especially the cellars, in which last there were two or three bottles of wine still left in a bin, covered with cobwebs, and evidently, by their appearance, undisturbed for many years. It was clear that the ghosts were not wine-bibbers.

For the rest, we discovered nothing of interest. There was a gloomy little backyard with very high walls. The stones of this yard were very damp—and what with the damp, and what with the dust and smoke-grime on the pavement, our feet left a slight impression where we passed. And now appeared the first strange phenomenon witnessed by myself in this strange abode. I saw, just before me, the print of a foot suddenly form itself, as it were. I stopped, caught hold of my servant, and pointed to it. In advance of that footprint as suddenly dropped another. We both saw it. I advanced quickly to the place; the footprint kept advancing before me, a small footprint—the foot of a child: the impression was too faint thoroughly to distinguish the shape, but it seemed to us both that it was the print of a naked foot. This phenomenon ceased when we arrived at the opposite wall, nor did it repeat itself on returning.

We remounted the stairs and entered the rooms on the ground floor, a dining parlour, a small back parlour, and a still smaller third room that had been probably appropriated to a footman—all still as death. We then visited the drawing rooms, which seemed fresh and new. In the front room, I seated myself in an armchair. F—— placed on the table the candlestick with which he had lighted us. I told him to shut the door. As he turned to do so, a chair opposite to me moved from the wall quickly and noiselessly and dropped itself about a yard from my own chair, immediately fronting it.

"Why, this is better than the turning-tables," said I, with a half-laugh—and as I laughed, my dog put back his head and howled.

F——, coming back, had not observed the movement of the chair. He employed himself now in stilling the dog. I continued to gaze at the chair and fancied I saw on it a pale blue misty outline of a human figure, but an outline so indistinct that I could only distrust my own vision. The dog was now quiet. "Put back that chair opposite to me," said I to F——; "put it back to the wall."

F—— obeyed. "Was that you, sir?" said he, turning abruptly.

"I—what!"

"Why, something struck me. I felt it sharply on the shoulder—just here."

"No," said I. "But we have jugglers present, and though we may not discover their tricks, we shall catch them before they frighten us."

We did not stay long in the drawing rooms—in fact, they felt so damp and so chilly that I was glad to get to the fire upstairs. We locked the doors of the drawing rooms—a precaution which, I should observe, we had taken with all the rooms we had searched below. The bedroom my servant had selected for me was the best on the floor—a large one with two windows fronting the street. The four-posted bed, which took up no inconsiderable space, was opposite to the fire, which burned clear and bright; a door in the wall to the left, between the bed and the window, communicated with the room, which my servant appropriated to himself.

This last was a small room with a sofa bed and had no communication with the landing place—no other door but that which conducted to the bedroom I was to occupy. On either side of my fireplace was a cupboard, without locks, flushed with the wall and covered with the same dull-brown paper. We examined these cupboards—only hooks to suspend female dresses—nothing else; we sounded the walls—evidently solid—the outer walls of the building. Having finished the survey of these apartments, warmed myself a few moments, and lighted my cigar, I then, still accompanied by F——, went forth to complete my reconnoitre. In the landing- place, there was another door; it was closed firmly. "Sir," said my servant in surprise, "I unlocked this door with all the others when I first came; it cannot have got locked from the inside, for it is a—"

Before he had finished his sentence, the door which neither of us then was touching, opened quietly of itself. We looked at each other for a single instant. The same thought seized both—some human agency might be detected here. I rushed in first; my servant followed. A small blank dreary room without furniture—a few empty boxes and hampers in a corner—a small window—the shutters closed—not even a fireplace—no other door but that by which we had entered—no carpet on the floor and the floor seemed very old, uneven, worm-eaten, mended here and there, as was shown by the whiter patches on the wood; but no living being, and no visible place in which a living being could have hidden. As we stood gazing around, the door by which we had entered closed as quietly as it had before opened: we were imprisoned.

For the first time, I felt a creep of undefinable horror. Not so, my servant. "Why, they don't think to trap us, sir; I could break that trumpery door with a kick of my foot."

"Try first if it will open to your hand," said I, shaking off the vague apprehension that had seized me, "while I open the shutters and see what is without."

I unbarred the shutters—the window looked on the little backyard I have before described; there was no ledge without—nothing but sheer descent. No man getting out of that window would have found any footing till he had fallen on the stones below.

F——, meanwhile, was vainly attempting to open the door. He now turned round to me and asked my permission to use force. And I should here state, in justice to the servant, that, far from evincing any superstitious terrors, his nerve, composure, and even gaiety amidst circumstances so extraordinary compelled my admiration and made me congratulate myself on having secured a companion in every way fitted to the occasion. I willingly gave him the permission he required. But though he was a remarkably strong man, his force was as idle as his milder efforts; the door did not even shake to his stoutest kick. Breathless and panting, he desisted. I then tried the door myself, equally in vain.

As I ceased the effort, again that creep of horror came over me; but this time, it was more cold and more stubborn. I felt as if some strange and ghastly exhalation were rising up from the chinks of that rugged floor and filling the atmosphere with a venomous influence hostile to human life. The door now very slowly and quietly opened of its own accord. We precipitated ourselves into the landing place. We both saw a large pale light—as large as the human figure but shapeless and unsubstantial—move before us, and ascend the stairs that led from the landing into the attics. I followed the light, and my servant followed me. It entered, to the right of the landing, a small garret, of which the door stood open. I entered in the same instant. The light then collapsed into a small globule, exceedingly brilliant and vivid; it rested a moment on a bed in the corner, quivered, and vanished. We approached the bed and examined it—a half-tester, such as is commonly found in attics devoted to servants. On the drawers that stood near it we perceived an old faded silk kerchief, with the needle still left in a rent half repaired. The kerchief was covered with dust; probably, it had belonged to the old woman who had last died in that house, and this might have been her sleeping room.

I had sufficient curiosity to open the drawers; there were a few odds and ends of the female dress and two letters tied round with a narrow ribbon of faded yellow. I took the liberty to possess myself of the letters. We found nothing else in the room worth noticing—nor did the light reappear, but we distinctly heard, as we turned to go, a pattering footfall on the floor—just before us. We went through the other attics (in all four), the footfall still preceding us. Nothing to be seen—nothing but the footfall heard. I had the letters in my hand; just as I was descending the stairs, I distinctly felt my wrist seized and a faint, soft effort made to draw the letters from my clasp. I only held them the more tightly, and the effort ceased.

We regained the bed chamber appropriated to me, and I then remarked that my dog had not followed us when we had left it. He was thrusting himself close to the fire and trembling. I was impatient to examine the letters; and while I read them, my servant opened a little box in which he had deposited the weapons I had ordered him to bring, took them out, placed them on a table close at my bed-head, and then occupied himself in soothing the dog, who, however, seemed to heed him very little.

The letters were short—they were dated; the dates exactly thirty-five years ago. They were evidently from a lover to his mistress or a husband to some young wife. Not only the terms of expression but a distinct reference to a former voyage indicated the writer to have been a seafarer. The spelling and handwriting were those of a man imperfectly educated, but still, the language itself was forcible. In the expressions of endearment, there was a kind of rough wild love; but here and there were dark unintelligible hints at some secret not of love—some secret that seemed of crime. "We ought to love each other," was one of the sentences I remember, "for how everyone else would execrate us if all was known." Again: "Don't let anyone be in the same room with you at night—you talk in your sleep." And again: "What's done can't be undone; and I tell you there's nothing against us unless the dead could come to life." Here there was underlined in better handwriting (a female's), "They do!" At the end of the letter, latest in the date, the same female hand had written these words: "Lost at sea the 4th of June, the same day as—"

I put down the letters and began to muse over their contents.

Fearing, however, that the train of thought into which I fell might unsteady my nerves, I fully determined to keep my mind in a fit state to cope with whatever marvellous the advancing night might bring forth. I roused myself—

laid the letters on the table—stirred up the fire, which was still bright and cheering—and opened my volume of Macaulay. I read quietly enough till about half-past eleven. I then threw myself dressed upon the bed and told my servant he might retire to his own room but must keep himself awake. I bade him to leave open the door between the two rooms. Thus alone, I kept two candles burning on the table by my bedhead. I placed my watch beside the weapons and calmly resumed my Macaulay.

Opposite to me, the fire burned clear and on the hearth rug, seemingly asleep, lay the dog. In about twenty minutes, I felt an exceedingly cold air pass by my cheek like a sudden draught. I fancied the door to my right, communicating with the landing place, must have got open, but no—it was closed. I then turned my glance to my left and saw the flame of the candles violently swayed as by a wind. At the same moment, the watch beside the revolver softly slid from the table—softly, softly—no visible hand—it was gone. I sprang up, seizing the revolver with one hand, the dagger with the other; I was not willing that my weapons should share the fate of the watch. Thus armed, I looked round the floor—no sign of the watch. Three slow, loud, distinct knocks were now heard at the bedhead; my servant called out, "Is that you, sir?"

"No; be on your guard."

The dog now roused himself and sat on his haunches, his ears moving quickly backwards and forwards. He kept his eyes fixed on me with a look so strange that he concentrated all my attention on himself. Slowly he rose up, all his hair bristling and stood perfectly rigid and with the same wild stare. I had no time, however, to examine the dog. Presently my servant emerged from his room, and if ever I saw the horror in the human face, it was then. I should not have recognized him whether we had met in the streets, so altered was every lineament. He passed by me quickly, saying in a whisper that seemed scarcely to come from his lips, "Run—run! it is after me!" He gained the door to the landing, pulled it open, and rushed forth. I followed him into the landing involuntarily, calling him to stop, but, without heeding me, he bounded down the stairs, clinging to the balusters and taking several steps at a time. I heard, where I stood, the street door open—heard it again clap to. I was left alone in the haunted house.

It was but for a moment that I remained undecided whether or not to follow my servant; pride and curiosity alike forbade so dastardly a flight. I re-entered my room, closing the door after me, and proceeded cautiously into the interior chamber. I encountered nothing to justify my servant's terror. I again carefully examined the walls to see if there were any concealed doors. I could find no trace of one—not even a seam in the dull-brown paper with which the room was hung. How, then, had the Thing, whatever it was, which had so scared him, obtained ingress except through my own chamber?

I returned to my room, shut and locked the door that opened upon the interior one, and stood on the hearth, expectant and prepared. I now perceived that the dog had slunk into an angle of the wall and was pressing himself close against it as if literally trying to force his way into it. I approached the animal and spoke to it; the poor brute was evidently beside itself with terror. It showed all its teeth, the slaver dropping from its jaws, and would certainly have bitten me if I had touched it. It did not seem to recognize me. Whoever has seen at the Zoological Gardens a rabbit fascinated by a serpent cowering in a corner may form some idea of the anguish that the dog exhibited. Finding all efforts to soothe the animal in vain, and fearing that his bite might be as venomous in that state as if in the madness of hydrophobia, I left him alone, placed my weapons on the table beside the fire, seated myself, and recommenced my Macaulay.

Perhaps in order not to appear seeking credit for courage, or rather a coolness, which the reader may conceive I exaggerate, I may be pardoned if I pause to indulge in one or two egotistical remarks.

As I hold the presence of mind, or what is called courage, to be precisely proportioned to familiarity with the circumstance that leads to it, so I should say that I had been long sufficiently familiar with all experiments that appertain to the Marvellous. I had witnessed many very extraordinary phenomena in various parts of the world— phenomena that would be either totally disbelieved if I stated them or ascribed to supernatural agencies. Now, my theory is that the Supernatural is the Impossible and that what is called supernatural is only something in the laws of nature of which we have been hitherto ignorant. Therefore, if a ghost rises before me, I have no right to say, "So, then, the supernatural is possible," but rather, "So, then, the apparition of a ghost is, contrary to received opinion, within the laws of nature—i.e. not supernatural."

Now, in all that I had hitherto witnessed, and indeed in all the wonders which the amateurs of mystery in our age record as facts, a material living agency is always required. On the Continent, you will still find magicians who assert that they can raise spirits. Assume for the moment that they assert truly, still the living material form of the magician is present, and he is the material agency by which from some constitutional peculiarities, certain strange phenomena are represented to your natural senses.

Accept again, as truthful, the tales of Spirit Manifestation in America—musical or other sounds— writings on paper, produced by no discernible hand— articles of furniture moved without apparent human agency—or the actual sight and touch of hands, to which no bodies seem to belong—still there must be found the medium or living being, with constitutional peculiarities capable of obtaining these signs. In fine, in all such marvels, supposing even that there is no imposture, there must be a human being like ourselves, by whom, or through whom, the effects presented to human beings are produced. It is so with the now familiar phenomena of mesmerism or electro-biology; the mind of the person operated on is affected through a material living agent. Nor, supposing it true that a mesmerised patient can respond to the will or passes of a mesmeriser a hundred miles distant, is the response less occasioned by a material being; it may be through a material fluid—call it Electric, call it Odic, call it what you will—which has the power of traversing space and passing obstacles, that the material effect is communicated from one to the other.

Hence all that I had hitherto witnessed, or expected to witness, in this strange house, I believed to be occasioned through some agency or medium as mortal as myself; and this idea necessarily prevented the awe with which those who regard as supernatural things that are not within the ordinary operations of nature, might have been impressed by the adventures of that memorable night.

As, then, it was my conjecture that all that was presented, or would be presented, to my senses, must originate in some human being gifted by the constitution with the power to present them and having some motive so to do, I felt an interest in my theory which, in its way, was rather philosophical than superstitious. And I can sincerely say that I was in as tranquil a temper for observation as any practical experimentalist could be in awaiting the effects of some rare though perhaps perilous, chemical combination. Of course, the more I kept my mind detached from fancy, the more the temper fitted for observation would be obtained; and I, therefore, riveted eye and thought on the strong daylight sense in the page of my Macaulay.

I now became aware that something interposed between the page and the light—the page was overshadowed; I looked up, and I saw what I should find very difficult, perhaps impossible, to describe.

It was a Darkness shaping itself out of the air in a very undefined outline. I cannot say it was of a human form, and yet it had more resemblance to a human form, or rather shadow, than anything else. As it stood, wholly apart and distinct from the air and the light around it, its dimensions seemed gigantic, the summit nearly touching the ceiling. While I gazed, a feeling of intense cold seized me. An iceberg before me could not more have chilled me, nor could the cold of an iceberg have been more purely physical. I feel convinced that it was not the cold caused by fear. As I continued to gaze, I thought—but this I cannot say with precision—that I distinguished two eyes looking down on me from the height. One moment I seemed to distinguish them clearly. The next, they seemed gone; but still, two rays of a pale-blue light frequently shot through the darkness, as from the height on which I half-believed, half-doubted, that I had encountered the eyes.

I strove to speak—my voice utterly failed me; I could only think to myself, "Is this fear? it is not fear!" I strove to rise—in vain; I felt as if weighed down by an irresistible force. Indeed, my impression was that of an immense and overwhelming Power opposed to my volition; that sense of utter inadequacy to cope with a force beyond men's, which one may feel physically in a storm at sea, in a conflagration, or when confronting some terrible wild beast, or rather, perhaps, the shark of the ocean, I felt moral. Opposed to my will was another will, as far superior to its strength as storm, fire, and shark are superior in material force to the force of men.

And now, as this impression grew on me, now came, at last, horror—horror to the degree that no words can convey. Still, I retained pride, if not courage; and in my own mind, I said, "This is horror, but it is not fear; unless I fear, I cannot be harmed; my reason rejects this thing; it is an illusion—I do not fear." With a violent effort, I succeeded at last in stretching out my hand towards the weapon on the table; as I did so, on the arm and shoulder, I received a strange shock, and my arm fell to my side, powerless. And now, to add to my horror, the light began slowly to wane from the candles—they were not, as it were, extinguished, but their flame seemed very gradually withdrawn; it was the same with the fire—the light was extracted from the fuel; in a few minutes the room was in utter darkness.

The dread that came over me, to be thus in the dark with that dark Thing, whose power was so intensely felt, brought a reaction of nerve. In fact, terror had reached that climax, that either my senses must have deserted me, or I must have burst through the spell. I did burst through it. I found the voice, though the voice was a shriek. I remember that I broke forth with words like these—"I do not fear, my soul does not fear",; and at the same time, I found the strength to rise. Still, in that profound gloom, I rushed to one of the windows—tore aside the curtain—flung open the shutters; my first thought was—light. And when I saw the moon high, clear, and calm, I felt a joy that almost compensated for the previous terror. There was the moon, and there was also the light from the gas lamps in the deserted, slumberous street. I turned to look back into the room; the moon penetrated its shadow very palely and partially—but still, there was light. The dark Thing, whatever it might be, was gone—except that I could yet see a dim shadow which seemed the shadow of that shade against the opposite wall.

My eye now rested on the table, and from under the table (which was without cloth or cover—an old mahogany round table), there rose a hand, visible as far as the wrist. It was a hand, seemingly, as much of flesh and blood as my own, but the hand of an aged person—lean, wrinkled, small too—a woman's hand.

That hand very softly closed on the two letters that lay on the table: hand and letters both vanished. There then came the same three loud, measured knocks I had heard at the bedhead before this extraordinary drama had commenced.

As those sounds slowly ceased, I felt the whole room vibrate sensibly; and at the far end, there rose, as from the floor, sparks or globules like bubbles of light, many-colored —green, yellow, fire-red, azure. Up and down, to and fro, hither, thither, as tiny will-o'-the-wisps, the sparks moved, slow or swift, each at its own caprice. A chair (as in the drawing room below) was now advanced from the wall without apparent agency and placed at the opposite side of the table. Suddenly, as forth from the chair, there grew a shape—a woman's shape. It was distinct as a shape of life —ghastly as a shape of death. The face was that of youth, with a strange, mournful beauty; the throat and shoulders were bare, the rest of the form in a loose robe of cloudy white. It began sleeking its long yellow hair, which fell over its shoulders; its eyes were not turned towards me but to the door; it seemed listening, watching, waiting. The shadow of the shade in the background grew darker, and again I thought I beheld the eyes gleaming out from the summit of the shadow—eyes fixed upon that shape.

As if from the door, though it did not open, there grew out another shape equally distinct, equally ghastly—a man's shape—a young man's. It was in the dress of the last century, or rather in a likeness of such dress; for both the male shape and the female, though defined, were evidently unsubstantial, impalpable—simulacra—phantasms; and there was something incongruous, grotesque, yet fearful, in contrast between the elaborate finery, the courtly precision of that old-fashioned garb, with its ruffles and lace and buckles, and the corpse-like aspect and ghost-like stillness of the flitting wearer. Just as the male shape approached the female, the dark Shadow started from the wall, all three for a moment wrapped in darkness. When the pale light returned, the two phantoms were as if in the grasp of the Shadow that towered between them; there was a bloodstain on the breast of the female, and the phantom male was leaning on its phantom sword, and blood seemed to trickle fast from the ruffles, from the lace; and the darkness of the intermediate Shadow swallowed them up —they were gone. And again, the bubbles of light shot sailed and undulated, growing thicker and thicker and more wildly confused in their movements.

The closet door to the right of the fireplace now opened, and from the aperture, there came the form of a woman aged. In her hand, she held letters—the very letters over which I had seen the Hand close; and behind her, I heard a footstep. She turned round as if to listen, then she opened the letters and seemed to read, and over her shoulder, I saw a livid face, the face as of a man long drowned—bloated, bleached—seaweed tangled in its dripping hair; and at her feet lay a form as of a corpse and beside the corpse there cowered a child, a miserable, squalid child, with famine in its cheeks and fear in its eyes. And as I looked in the old woman's face, the wrinkles and lines vanished, and it became a face of youth—hard-eyed, stony, but still youth; and the Shadow darted forth and darkened over these phantoms as it had darkened over the last.

Nothing now was left but the Shadow, and on that, my eyes were intently fixed, till again eyes grew out of the Shadow—malignant, serpent eyes. And the bubbles of light again rose and fell, and in their disordered, irregular, turbulent maze, mingled with the wan moonlight. And now from these globules themselves as from the shell of an egg, monstrous things burst out; the air grew filled with them; larvæ so bloodless and so hideous that I can in no way describe them except to remind the reader of the swarming life which the solar microscope brings before his eyes in a drop of water—things transparent, supple, agile, chasing each other, devouring each other—forms like nought ever beheld by the naked eye. As the shapes were without symmetry, their movements were without order. In their very vagrancies, there was no sport; they came round me and round, thicker and faster and swifter, swarming over my head, crawling over my right arm, which was outstretched in involuntary command against all evil beings.

Sometimes I felt touched, but not by them; invisible hands touched me. Once I felt the clutch as of cold soft fingers at my throat. I was still equally conscious that if I gave way to fear, I should be in bodily peril, and I concentrated all my faculties on the single focus of resisting stubborn will. And I turned my sight from the Shadow— above all, from those strange serpent eyes—eyes that had now become distinctly visible. For there, though in nought else around me, I was aware that there was a will, and a will of intense, creative, working evil, which might crush down my own.

The pale atmosphere in the room began now to redden as if in the air of some near conflagration. The larvæ grew lurid as things that live in fire. Again the room vibrated; again were heard the three measured knocks; and again, all things were swallowed up in the darkness of the dark Shadow, as if out of that darkness all had come, into that darkness all returned.

As the gloom receded, the Shadow was wholly gone. Slowly as it had been withdrawn, the flame grew again into the candles on the table, again into the fuel in the grate. The whole room came once more calmly, healthfully into sight.

The two doors were still closed, the door communicating with the servant's room still locked. In the corner of the wall, into which he had so convulsively niched himself, lay the dog. I called to him—no movement; I approached—the animal was dead; his eyes protruded; his tongue out of his mouth; the froth gathered round his jaws. I took him in my arms; I brought him to the fire; I felt acute grief for the loss of my poor favourite—acute self-reproach; I accused myself of his death; I imagined he had died of fright. But what was my surprise on finding that his neck was actually broken—actually twisted out of the vertebræ? Had this been done in the dark?—must it not have been by a hand human as mine?—must there not have been a human agency all the while in that room? That is a good cause to suspect it. I cannot tell. I cannot do more than state the fact fairly; the reader may draw his own inference.

Another surprising circumstance—my watch was restored to the table from which it had been so mysteriously withdrawn, but it had stopped at the very moment it was so withdrawn; nor, despite all the skill of the watchmaker, has it ever gone since—that is, it will go in a strange erratic way for a few hours, and then comes to a dead stop—it is worthless.

Nothing more chanced for the rest of the night. Nor, indeed, had I long to wait before the dawn broke. Not till it was broad daylight did I quit the haunted house. Before I did so, I revisited the little blind room in which my servant and myself had been for a time imprisoned. I had a strong impression—for which I could not account—that from that room had originated the mechanism of the phenomena—if I may use the term—which had been experienced in my chamber. And though I entered it now in the clear day, with the sun peering through the filmy window, I still felt, as I stood on its floor, the creep of the horror which I had first there experienced the night before and which had been so aggravated by what had passed in my chamber. I could not, indeed, bear to stay more than half a minute within those walls. I descended the stairs, and again I heard the footfall before me; when I opened the street door, I thought I could distinguish a very low laugh. I gained my own home, expecting to find my runaway servant there. But he had not presented himself, nor did I hear more of him for three days, when I received a letter from him, dated from Liverpool, to this effect:—

"Honoured Sir,—I humbly entreat your pardon, though I can scarcely hope that you will think I deserve it, unless—which Heaven forbid!—you saw what I did. I feel that it will be years before I can recover myself, and as to being fit for service, it is out of the question. I am therefore going to my brother-in-law at Melbourne. The ship sails tomorrow. Perhaps the long voyage may set me up. I do nothing now but start and tremble, and fancy It is behind me. I humbly beg you, honoured sir, to order my clothes, and whatever wages are due to me, to be sent to my mother's, at Walworth—John knows her address."

The letter ended with additional apologies, somewhat incoherent, and explanatory details as to the effects that had been under the writer's charge.

This flight may perhaps warrant a suspicion that the man wished to go to Australia and had been somehow or other fraudulently mixed up with the events of the night. I say nothing in refutation of that conjecture; rather, I suggest it as one that would seem to many persons the most probable solution of improbable occurrences. My own theory remained unshaken. I returned in the evening to the house to bring away in a hack cab the things I had left there, with my poor dog's body. In this task, I was not disturbed, nor did any incident worth note befall me, except that still, on ascending and descending the stairs, I heard the same footfall in advance. On leaving the house, I went to Mr J——'s. He was at home. I returned him the keys, told him that my curiosity was sufficiently gratified, and was about to relate quickly what had passed when he stopped me and said, though with much politeness, that he had no longer any interest in a mystery which none had ever solved.

I determined at least to tell him of the two letters I had read, as well as of the extraordinary manner in which they had disappeared, and I then inquired if he thought they had been addressed to the woman who had died in the house and if there were anything in her early history which could possibly confirm the dark suspicions to which the letters gave rise. Mr J—— seemed startled and, after musing a few moments, answered, "I know but little of the woman's earlier history, except, as I before told you, that her family were known to mine. But you revive some vague reminiscences to her prejudice. I will make inquiries, and inform you of their result. Still, even if we could admit the popular superstition that a person who had been either the perpetrator or the victim of dark crimes in life could revisit, as a restless spirit, the scene in which those crimes had been committed, I should observe that the house was infested by strange sights and sounds before the old woman died—you smile—what would you say?"

"I would say this, that I am convinced, if we could get to the bottom of these mysteries, we should find a living human agency."

"What! you believe it is all an imposture? For what object?"

"Not an imposture in the ordinary sense of the word. If suddenly I were to sink into a deep sleep, from which you could not awake me, but in that sleep could answer questions with an accuracy which I could not pretend to when awake—tell you what money you had in your pocket

—nay, describe your very thoughts—it is not necessarily an imposture, any more than it is necessarily supernatural. I should be, unconsciously to myself, under a mesmeric influence, conveyed to me from a distance by a human being who had acquired power over me by previous rapport."

"Granting mesmerism, so far carried, to be a fact, you are right. And you would infer from this that a mesmeriser might produce the extraordinary effects you and others have witnessed over inanimate objects—fill the air with sights and sounds?"

"Or impress our senses with the belief in them—we never having been en rapport with the person acting on us? No. What is commonly called mesmerism could not do this; but there may be a power akin to mesmerism, and superior to it—the power that in the old days was called Magic. That such a power may extend to all inanimate objects of matter, I do not say; but if so, it would not be against nature, only a rare power in nature which might be given to constitutions with certain peculiarities and cultivated by practice to an extraordinary degree. That such a power might extend over the dead—that is, over certain thoughts and memories that the dead may still retain—and compel, not that which ought properly to be called the soul, and which is far beyond human reach, but rather a phantom of what has been most earth-stained on earth, to make itself apparent to our senses—is a very ancient though obsolete theory, upon which I will hazard no opinion. But I do not conceive the power would be supernatural.

"Let me illustrate what I mean from an experiment which Paracelsus describes as not difficult and which the author of the Curiosities of Literature cites as credible: A flower perishes; you burn it. Whatever were the elements of that flower while it lived are gone, dispersed. You know not whither; you can never discover nor re-collect them. But you can, by chemistry, out of the burnt dust of that flower, raise a spectrum of the flower, just as it seemed in life. It may be the same with the human being. The soul has so much escaped you as the essence or elements of the flower. Still, you may make a spectrum of it. And this phantom, though in the popular superstition it is held to be the soul of the departed, must not be confounded with the true soul; it is but the eidolon of the dead form.

"Hence, like the best-attested stories of ghosts or spirits, the thing that most strikes us is the absence of what we hold to be soul—that is, of superior emancipated intelligence. They come for little or no object—they seldom speak, if they do come; they utter no ideas above that of an ordinary person on earth. These American spirit-seers have published volumes of communications in prose and verse, which they assert to be given in the names of the most illustrious dead—Shakespeare, Bacon—heaven knows whom. Those communications, taking the best, are certainly not a whit of a higher order than would be communications from living persons of fair talent and education; they are wondrously inferior to what Bacon, Shakespeare, and Plato said and wrote when on earth.

"Nor, what is more notable, do they ever contain an idea that was not on the earth before. Wonderful, therefore, as such phenomena may be (granting them to be truthful), I see much that philosophy may question, nothing that it is incumbent on philosophy to deny—viz. nothing supernatural. They are, but ideas are conveyed somehow or other (we have not yet discovered the means) from one mortal brain to another. Whether, in so doing, tables walk of their own accord, fiend-like shapes appear in a magic circle, bodyless hands rise and remove material objects, or a Thing of Darkness, such as presented itself to me, freezes our blood—still am I persuaded that these are but agencies conveyed, as by electric wires, to my own brain from the brain of another. In some constitutions, there is a natural chemistry, and those may produce chemic wonders—in others, a natural fluid call it electricity, and these produce electric wonders. But they differ in this from Normal Science—they are alike objectless, purposeless, puerile, and frivolous. They lead on to no grand results, and therefore, the world does not heed, and true sages have not cultivated them. But sure I am that of all I saw or heard, a man, human as myself was the remote originator, and I believe unconsciously to himself as to the exact effects produced, for this reason: no two persons, you say, have ever told you that they experienced exactly the same thing. Well, observe, no two persons ever experience exactly the same dream. If this were an ordinary imposture, the machinery would be arranged for results that would but little vary; if it were a supernatural agency permitted by the Almighty, it would surely be for some definite end.

"These phenomena belong to neither class; my persuasion is, that they originate in some brain now far distant; that that brain had no distinct volition in anything that occurred; that what does occur reflects but its devious, motley, ever-shifting, half-formed thoughts; in short, that it has been but the dreams of such a brain put into action and invested with a semi-substance. That this brain is of immense power, that it can set matter into movement, that it is malignant and destructive, I believe: some material force must have killed my dog; it might, for aught I know, have sufficed to kill myself, had I been as subjugated by terror as the dog—had my intellect or my spirit given me no countervailing resistance in my will."

"It killed your dog! that is fearful! indeed, it is strange that no animal can be induced to stay in that house; not even a cat. Rats and mice are never found in it."

"The instincts of the brute creation detect influences deadly to their existence. Man's reason has a sense less subtle, because it has a resisting power more supreme. But enough; do you comprehend my theory?"

"Yes, though imperfectly—and I accept any crotchet (pardon the word), however odd, rather than embrace at once the notion of ghosts and hobgoblins we imbibed in our nurseries. Still, to my unfortunate house the evil is the same. What on earth can I do with the house?"

"I will tell you what I would do. I am convinced from my own internal feelings that the small unfurnished room at right angles to the door of the bedroom which I occupied, forms a starting-point or receptacle for the influences which haunt the house; and I strongly advise you to have the walls opened, the floor removed—nay, the whole room pulled down. I observe that it is detached from the body of the house, built over the small back-yard, and could be removed without injury to the rest of the building."

"And you think, if I did that——"

"You would cut off the telegraph wires. Try it. I am so persuaded that I am right, that I will pay half the expense if you will allow me to direct the operations."

"Nay, I am well able to afford the cost; for the rest, allow me to write to you."

About ten days afterwards, I received a letter from Mr J——, telling me that he had visited the house since I had seen him; that he had found the two letters I had described, replaced in the drawer from which I had taken them; that he had read them with misgivings like my own; that he had instituted a cautious inquiry about the woman to whom I rightly conjectured they had been written. It seemed that thirty-six years ago (a year before the date of the letters), she had married, against the wish of her relatives, an American of very suspicious character; in fact, he was generally believed to have been a pirate. She herself was the daughter of very respectable tradespeople and had served in the capacity of a nursery governess before her marriage. She had a brother, a widower, who was considered wealthy, and who had one child of about six years old. A month after the marriage, the body of this brother was found in the Thames, near London Bridge; there seemed some marks of violence about his throat, but they were not deemed sufficient to warrant the inquest in any other verdict than that of "found drowned."

The American and his wife took charge of the little boy, the deceased brother having by his will left his sister the guardian of his only child—and in the event of the child's death, the sister inherited. The child died about six months afterwards—it was supposed to have been neglected and ill-treated. The neighbours deposed to have heard it shriek at night. The surgeon who had examined it after death said that it was emaciated as if from want of nourishment, and the body was covered with livid bruises. It seemed that one winter night, the child had sought to escape—crept out into the backyard—tried to scale the wall —fallen back exhausted and been found in the morning on the stones in a dying state. But though there was some evidence of cruelty, there was none of murder; and the aunt and her husband had sought to palliate cruelty by alleging the exceeding stubbornness and perversity of the child, who was declared to be half-witted. Be that as it may, at the orphan's death the aunt inherited her brother's fortune.

Before the first wedded year was out, the American quitted England abruptly and never returned to it. He obtained a cruising vessel, which was lost in the Atlantic two years afterwards. The widow was left in affluence, but reverses of various kinds had befallen her: a bank broke— an investment failed—she went into a small business and became insolvent—then she entered into service, sinking lower and lower, from housekeeper down to maid-of-all-work—never long retaining a place, though nothing peculiar against her character was ever alleged. She was considered sober, honest, and peculiarly quiet in her ways; still, nothing prospered with her. And so she had dropped into the workhouse, from which Mr J—— had taken her, to be placed in charge of the very house which she had rented as mistress in the first year of her wedded life.

Mr J—— added that he had passed an hour alone in the unfurnished room, which I had urged him to destroy and that his impressions of dread while there were so great, though he had neither heard nor seen anything, that he was eager to have the walls bared and the floors removed as I had suggested. He had engaged persons for the work and would commence any day I would name.

The day was accordingly fixed. I repaired to the haunted house—we went into the blind dreary room, took up the skirting, and then the floors. Under the rafters, covered with rubbish, was found a trap door quite large enough to admit a man. It was closely nailed down, with clamps and rivets of iron. On removing these, we descended into a room below, the existence of which had never been suspected. In this room, there had been a window and a flue, but they had been bricked over, evidently, for many years. With the help of candles, we examined this place; it still retained some mouldering furniture—three chairs, an oak settle, a table—all of the fashion of about eighty years ago. There was a chest of drawers against the wall, in which we found, half-rotted away, old-fashioned articles of a man's dress, such as might have been worn eighty or a hundred years ago by a gentleman of some rank—costly steel buckles and buttons, like those yet worn in court dresses—a handsome court sword—in a waistcoat which had once been rich with gold lace, but which was now blackened and foul with damp, we found five guineas, a few silver coins, and an ivory ticket, probably for some place of entertainment long since passed away. But our main discovery was in a kind of iron safe fixed to the wall, the lock of which it cost us much trouble to get picked.

In this safe were three shelves and two small drawers. Ranged on the shelves were several small bottles of crystal, hermetically stopped. They contained colorless volatile essences, of what nature I shall say no more than that they were not poisons—phosphor and ammonia entered into some of them. There were also some very curious glass tubes and a small pointed rod of iron, with a large lump of rock crystal and another of amber—also a loadstone of great power.

In one of the drawers, we found a miniature portrait set in gold, retaining the freshness of its colors most remarkably, considering the length of time it had probably been there. The portrait was that of a man who might be somewhat advanced in middle life, perhaps forty-seven or forty-eight.

It was a most peculiar face—a most impressive face. If you could fancy some mighty serpent transformed into man, preserving in the human lineaments the old serpent type, you would have a better idea of that countenance than long descriptions can convey: the width and flatness of frontal—the tapering elegance of contour disguising the strength of the deadly jaw—the long, large, terrible eye, glittering and green as the emerald—and withal a certain ruthless calm, as if from the consciousness of immense power. The strange thing was this—the instant I saw the miniature I recognized a startling likeness to one of the rarest portraits in the world—the portrait of a man of a rank only below that of royalty, who in his own day had made a considerable noise. History says little or nothing of him, but search the correspondence of his contemporaries, and you find reference to his wild daring, his bold profligacy, his restless spirit, his taste for the occult sciences. While still in the meridian of life, he died and was buried, so say the chronicles, in a foreign land. He died in time to escape the grasp of the law, for he was accused of crimes which would have given him to the headsman.

After his death, the portraits of him, which had been numerous, for he had been a munificent encourager of art, were bought up and destroyed—it was supposed by his heirs, who might have been glad, could they have razed his very name from their splendid line. He had enjoyed a vast wealth; a large portion of this was believed to have been embezzled by a favourite astrologer or soothsayer—at all events, it had unaccountably vanished at the time of his death. One portrait alone of him was supposed to have escaped the general destruction; I had seen it in the house of a collector some months before. It had made on me a wonderful impression, as it does on all who behold it—a face never to be forgotten, and there was that face in the miniature that lay within my hand. True, that in the miniature, the man was a few years older than in the portrait I had seen, or than the original was even at the time of his death. But a few years!—why, between the date in which flourished that direful noble and the date in which the miniature was evidently painted, there was an interval of more than two centuries. While I was thus gazing, silent and wondering, Mr J—— said:

"But is it possible? I have known this man."

"How—where?" I cried.

"In India. He was high in the confidence of the Rajah of ——, and wellnigh drew him into a revolt which would have lost the Rajah his dominions. The man was a Frenchman—his name de V——, clever, bold, lawless. We insisted on his dismissal and banishment: it must be the same man—no two faces like his—yet this miniature seems nearly a hundred years old."

Mechanically I turned round the miniature to examine the back of it, and on the back was engraved a pentacle; in the middle of the pentacle was a ladder, and the third step of the ladder was formed by the date 1765. Examining still more minutely, I detected a spring; this, on being pressed opened the back of the miniature as a lid. Withinside the lid was engraved "Mariana to thee—Be faithful in life and in death to ——." Here follows a name that I will not mention, but it was not unfamiliar to me. I had heard it spoken of by old men in my childhood as the name borne by a dazzling charlatan, who had made a great sensation in London for a year or so, and had fled the country on the charge of a double murder within his own house—that of his mistress and his rival. I said nothing of this to Mr J——, to whom reluctantly I resigned the miniature.

We had found no difficulty in opening the first drawer within the iron safe; we found great difficulty in opening the second: it was not locked, but it resisted all efforts till we inserted in the chinks the edge of a chisel. When we had thus drawn it forth, we found a very singular apparatus in the nicest order. Upon a small thin book, or rather tablet, was placed a saucer of crystal; this saucer was filled with a clear liquid—on that liquid floated a kind of compass, with a needle shifting rapidly round, but instead of the usual points of a compass were seven strange characters, not very unlike those used by astrologers to denote the planets. A very peculiar but not strong nor displeasing odour came from this drawer, which was lined with a wood that we afterwards discovered to be hazel. Whatever the cause of this odour, it produced a material effect on the nerves. We all felt it, even the two workmen who were in the room—a creeping tingling sensation from the tips of the fingers to the roots of the hair. Impatient to examine the tablet, I removed the saucer. As I did so the needle of the compass went round and round with exceeding swiftness, and I felt a shock that ran through my whole frame so that I dropped the saucer on the floor. The liquid was spilt—the saucer was broken—the compass rolled to the end of the room—and at that instant, the walls shook to and fro as if a giant had swayed and rocked them.

The two workmen were so frightened that they ran up the ladder by which we had descended from the trap door, but seeing that nothing more happened, they were easily induced to return.

Meanwhile, I had opened the tablet: it was bound in plain red leather with a silver clasp; it contained, but one sheet of thick vellum, and on that sheet were inscribed, within a double pentacle, words in old monkish Latin, which are literally to be translated thus:—"On all that it can reach within these walls—sentient or inanimate, living or dead—as moves the needle, so work my will! Accursed be the house, and restless be the dwellers therein."

We found no more. Mr J—— burnt the tablet and its anathema. He razed the foundations of the part of the building containing the secret room with the chamber over it. He had then the courage to inhabit the house himself for a month, and a quieter, better-conditioned house could not be found in all of London. Subsequently, he let it to his advantage, and his tenant made no complaints.

But my story is not yet done. A few days after Mr J—— had removed into the house, I paid him a visit. We were standing by the open window and conversing. A van containing some articles of furniture which he was moving from his former house was at the door. I had just urged on him my theory that all those phenomena regarded as supermundane had emanated from a human brain, adducing the charm, or rather curse, we had found and destroyed in support of my philosophy. Mr J—— was observing in reply, "That even if mesmerism, or whatever analogous power it might be called, could really thus work in the absence of the operator, and produce effects so extraordinary, still could those effects continue when the operator himself was dead? and if the spell had been wrought, and, indeed, the room walled up, more than seventy years ago, the probability was, that the operator had long since departed this life"; Mr J——, I say, was thus answering, when I caught hold of his arm and pointed to the street below.

A well-dressed man had crossed from the opposite side and was accosting the carrier in charge of the van. His face, as he stood, was exactly fronting our window. It was the face of the miniature we had discovered; it was the face of the portrait of the noble three centuries ago.

"Good Heavens!" cried Mr J——, "that is the face of de V——, and scarcely a day older than when I saw it in the Rajah's court in my youth!"

Seized by the same thought, we both hastened downstairs. I was first in the street, but the man had already gone. I caught sight of him, however, not many yards in advance, and in another moment, I was by his side.

I had resolved to speak to him, but when I looked into his face, I felt as if it were impossible to do so. That eye —the eye of the serpent—fixed and held me spellbound. And withal, about the man's whole person there was a dignity, an air of pride and station and superiority, that would have made anyone, habituated to the usages of the world, hesitate long before venturing upon liberty or impertinence. And what could I say? what was it, I would ask? Thus ashamed of my first impulse, I fell a few paces back, still, however, following the stranger, undecided about what else to do. Meanwhile, he turned the corner of the street; a plain carriage was in waiting, with a servant out of livery, dressed like a valet-de-place, at the carriage door. In another moment, he had stepped into the carriage, and it drove off. I returned to the house. Mr J—— was still at the street door. He had asked the carrier what the stranger had said to him.

"Merely asked whom that house now belonged to."

The same evening I happened to go with a friend to a place in town called the Cosmopolitan Club, a place open to men of all countries, all opinions, and all degrees. One orders one's coffee and smokes one's cigar. One is always sure to meet agreeable, sometimes remarkable, persons.

I had not been two minutes in the room before I beheld at a table, conversing with an acquaintance of mine, whom I will designate by the initial G——, the man—the Original of the Miniature. He was now without his hat, and the likeness was yet more startling, only I observed that while he was conversing, there was less severity in the countenance; there was even a smile, though a very quiet and very cold one. The dignity of mien I had acknowledged in the street was also more striking, a dignity akin to that which invests some prince of the East— conveying the idea of supreme indifference and habitual, indisputable, indolent, but resistless power.

G—— soon after left the stranger, who then took up a scientific journal, which seemed to absorb his attention.

I drew G—— aside. "Who and what is that gentleman?"

"That? Oh, a very remarkable man indeed. I met him last year amidst the caves of Petra—the scriptural Edom. He is the best Oriental scholar I know. We joined company, had an adventure with robbers, in which he showed a coolness that saved our lives; afterwards he invited me to spend a day with him in a house he had bought at Damascus—a house buried amongst almond blossoms and roses—the most beautiful thing! He had lived there for some years, quite as an Oriental, in grand style. I half suspect he is a renegade, immensely rich, very odd; by the by, a great mesmeriser. I have seen him with my own eyes produce an effect on inanimate things. If you take a letter from your pocket and throw it to the other end of the room, he will order it to come to his feet, and you will see the letter wriggle itself along the floor till it has obeyed his command. 'Pon my honour, 'tis true: I have seen him affect even the weather, disperse or collect clouds, by means of a glass tube or wand. But he does not like talking of these matters to strangers. He has only just arrived in England; says he has not been here for a great many years; let me introduce him to you."

"Certainly! He is English, then? What is his name?"

"Oh!—a very homely one—Richards."

"And what is his birth—his family?"

"How do I know? What does it signify?—no doubt some parvenu, but rich—so infernally rich!"

G—— drew me up to the stranger, and the introduction was effected. The manners of Mr Richards were not those of an adventurous traveller. Travellers are in general, constitutionally gifted with high animal spirits: they are talkative, eager, and imperious. Mr Richards was calm and subdued in tone, with manners which were made distant by the loftiness of punctilious courtesy—the manners of a former age. I observed that the English he spoke were not exactly of our day. I should even have said that the accent was slightly foreign. But then Mr Richards remarked that he had been little in the habit for many years of speaking in his native tongue. The conversation fell upon the changes in the aspect of London since he had last visited our metropolis. G—— then glanced off to the moral changes—literary, social, political—the great men who were removed from the stage within the last twenty years —the new great men who were coming on. In all this, Mr Richards evinced no interest. He had evidently read none of our living authors and seemed scarcely acquainted by name with our younger statesmen. Once and only once, he laughed; it was when G—— asked him whether he had any thoughts of getting into Parliament. And the laugh was inward—sarcastic—sinister—a sneer raised into a laugh. After a few minutes G—— left us to talk to some other acquaintances who had just lounged into the room, and I then said quietly:

"I have seen a miniature of you, Mr Richards, in the house you once inhabited, and perhaps built, if not wholly, at least in part, in —— Street. You passed by that house this morning."

Not till I had finished did I raise my eyes to his, and then his fixed my gaze so steadfastly that I could not withdraw it—those fascinating serpent eyes. But involuntarily, and if the words that translated my thought were dragged from me, I added in a low whisper, "I have been a student in the mysteries of life and nature; of those mysteries, I have known the occult professors. I have the right to speak to you thus." And I uttered a certain password.

"Well," said he dryly, "I concede the right—what would you ask?"

"To what extent human will in certain temperaments extend?"

"To what extent can be thought to extend? Think, and before you draw breath, you are in China!"

"True. But my thought has no power in China."

"Give it expression, and it may have: you may write down a thought which, sooner or later, may alter the whole condition of China. What is a law but a thought? Therefore thought is infinite—therefore, thought has power; not in proportion to its value—a bad thought may make a bad law as potent as a good thought can make a good one."

"Yes, what you say confirms my own theory. Through invisible currents, one human brain may transmit its ideas to other human brains with the same rapidity as a thought promulgated by visible means. And as thought is imperishable—as it leaves its stamp behind it in the natural world even when the thinker has passed out of this world —so the thought of the living may have the power to rouse up and revive the thoughts of the dead—such as those thoughts were in life—though the thought of the living cannot reach the thoughts which the dead now may entertain. Is it not so?"

"I decline to answer if, in my judgment, thought has the limit you would fix to it; but proceed. You have a special question you wish to put."

"Intense malignity in an intense will, engendered in a peculiar temperament, and aided by natural means within reach of science, may produce effects like those ascribed of old to evil magic. It might thus haunt the walls of human habitation with spectral revivals of all guilty thoughts and guilty deeds once conceived and done within those walls; all, in short, with which the evil will claims rapport and affinity—imperfect, incoherent, fragmentary snatches at the old dramas acted therein years ago. Thoughts thus crossing each other haphazardly, as in the nightmare of a vision, growing up into phantom sights and sounds, and all serving to create horror, not because those sights and sounds are really visitations from a world without, but that they are ghastly monstrous renewals of what has been in this world itself, set into malignant play by a malignant mortal.

"And it is through the material agency of that human brain that these things would acquire even a human power—would strike as with the shock of electricity, and might kill, if the thought of the person assailed did not rise superior to the dignity of the original assailer—might kill the most powerful animal if unnerved by fear, but not injure the feeblest man, if, while his flesh crept, his mind stood out fearless. Thus, when in old stories we read of a magician rented to pieces by the fiends he had evoked—or still more, in Eastern legends, that one magician succeeds by arts in destroying another—there may be so far truth that a material being has clothed, from its own evil propensities certain elements and fluids, usually quiescent or harmless, with awful shape and terrific force—just as the lightning that had lain hidden and innocent in the cloud becomes by natural law suddenly visible, takes a distinct shape to the eye, and can strike destruction on the object to which it is attracted."

"You are not without glimpses of a very mighty secret," said Mr Richards, composedly. "According to your view, could a mortal obtain the power you speak of, he would necessarily be a malignant and evil being."

"If the power were exercised as I have said, most malignant and most evil—though I believe in the ancient traditions that he could not injure the good. His will could only injure those with whom it has established an affinity or over whom it forces unresisted sway. I will now imagine an example that may be within the laws of nature yet seem wild as the fables of a bewildered monk.

"You will remember that Albertus Magnus, after describing minutely the process by which spirits may be invoked and commanded, adds emphatically that the process will instruct and avail only to the few—that a man must be born a magician!—that is, born with a peculiar physical temperament, as a man is born a poet. Rarely are men in whose constitution lurks this occult power of the highest order of intellect;—usually, in the intellect, there is some twist, perversity, or disease. But, on the other hand, they must possess, to an astonishing degree, the faculty to concentrate thought on a single object—the energic faculty that we call will. Therefore, though their intellect is not sound, it is exceedingly forcible for the attainment of what it desires. I will imagine such a person, pre-eminently gifted with this constitution and its concomitant forces. I will place him in the loftier grades of society. I will suppose his desires emphatically those of the sensualist—he has, therefore, a strong love of life. He is an absolute egotist— his will is concentrated in himself—he has fierce passions— he knows no enduring, no holy affections, but he can covet eagerly what for the moment he desires—he can hate implacably what opposes itself to his objects—he can commit fearful crimes, yet feel small remorse—he resorts rather to curses upon others than to penitence for his misdeeds. Circumstances to which his constitution guides him lead him to a rare knowledge of the natural secrets which may serve his egotism. He is a close observer, and his passions encourage observation. He is a minute calculator, not from a love of truth, but where the love of self sharpens his faculties—therefore, he can be a man of science.

"I suppose such a being, having by experience learned the power of his arts over others, trying what may be the power of will over his own frame, and studying all that in natural philosophy may increase that power. He loves life. He dreads death; he wills to live on. He cannot restore himself to youth, he cannot entirely stay the progress of death, he cannot make himself immortal in flesh and blood, but he may arrest for a time so prolonged as to appear incredible if I said it—that hardening of the parts which constitutes old age. A year may age him no more than an hour ages another. His intense will, scientifically trained into system, operates, in short, over the wear and tear of his own frame. He lives on. That he may not seem a portent and a miracle, he dies from time to time, seemingly, to certain persons. Having schemed the transfer of a wealth that suffices to his wants, he disappears from one corner of the world and contrives that his obsequies shall be celebrated. He reappears at another corner of the world, where he resides undetected, and does not revisit the scenes of his former career till all who could remember his features are no more. He would be profoundly miserable if he had affections—he has none but for himself. No good man would accept his longevity, and to no men, good or bad, would he or could he communicate its true secret. Such a man might exist; such a man as I have described I see now before me!—Duke of ——, in the court of ——, dividing time between lust and brawl, alchemists and wizards;—again, in the last century, charlatan and criminal, with a nameless noble, domiciled in the house at which you gazed to-day, and flying from the law you had outraged, none knew whither; traveller once more revisiting London, with the same earthly passions which filled your heart when races now no more walked through yonder streets; outlaw from the school of all the nobler and diviner mystics; execrable Image of Life in Death and Death in Life, I warn you back from the cities and homes of healthful men; back to the ruins of departed empires; back to the deserts of nature unredeemed!"

There answered me a whisper so musical, so potently musical, that it seemed to enter into my whole being and subdue me despite myself. Thus it said:

"I have sought one like you for the last hundred years. Now I have found you. We part not till I know what

I desire. The vision that sees through the Past, and cleaves through the veil of the Future, is in you at this hour; never before, never to come again. The vision of no puling fantastic girl, of no sick-bed somnambule, but of a strong man, with a vigorous brain. Soar and look forth!"

As he spoke, I felt as if I rose out of myself upon eagle wings. All the weight seemed gone from the air—roofless the room, roofless the dome of space. I was not in the body —where I knew not—but aloft over time, over the earth.

Again I heard the melodious whisper,—"You say right. I have mastered great secrets by the power of Will; true, by Will and by Science I can retard the process of years: but death comes not by age alone. Can I frustrate the accidents which bring death upon the young?"

"No; every accident is a providence. Before a providence snaps every human will."

"Shall I die at last, ages and ages hence, by the slow, though inevitable, growth of time, or by the cause that I call accident?"

"By a cause you call accident."

"Is not the end still remote?" asked the whisper, with a slight tremor.

"Regarded as my life regards, time it is still remote."

"And shall I, before then, mix with the world of men as I did ere I learned these secrets, resume eager interest in their strife and their trouble—battle with ambition, and use the power of the sage to win the power that belongs to kings?"

"You will yet play a part on the earth that will fill earth, with commotion and amaze. For wondrous designs have you, a wonder yourself, been permitted to live on through the centuries. All the secrets you have stored will then have their uses—all that now makes you a stranger amidst the generations will contribute then to make you their lord. As the trees and the straws are drawn into a whirlpool—as they spin round, are sucked to the deep, and again tossed aloft by the eddies, so shall races and thrones be plucked into the charm of your vortex. Awful Destroyer —but in destroying, made, against your own will, a Constructor!"

"And that date, too, is far off?"

"Far off; when it comes, think your end in this world is at hand!"

"How and what is the end? Look east, west, south, and north."

"In the north, where you never yet trod towards the point whence your instincts have warned you, there a spectre will seize you. 'Tis Death! I see a ship—it is haunted —'tis chased—it sails on. Baffled navies sail after that ship. It enters the region of ice. It passes a sky red with meteors. Two moons stand on high over ice reefs. I see the ship locked between white defiles—they are ice rocks. I see the dead strew the decks—stark and livid, green mould on their limbs. All are dead but one man—it is you! But years, though so slowly they come, have then scathed you. There is the coming of age on your brow, and the will is relaxed in the cells of the brain. Still, that will, though enfeebled, exceeds all that man knew before you, through the will you live on, gnawed with famine; and nature no longer obeys you in that death-spreading region; the sky is a sky of iron, and the air has iron clamps and the ice-rocks wedge in the ship. Hark how it cracks and groans. Ice will imbed it as amber embeds a straw. And a man has gone forth, living yet, from the ship and its dead; and he has clambered up the spikes of an iceberg, and the two moons gaze down on his form. That man is yourself, and terror is on you—terror, and terror has swallowed your will. And I see swarming up the steep ice-rock, grey grisly things. The bears of the north have scented their quarry—they come near you and nearer, shambling and rolling their bulk. And in that day, every moment shall seem to you longer than the centuries through which you have passed. And heed this—the afterlife moments continue to make the bliss or the hell of eternity."

"Hush," said the whisper, "but the day, you assure me, is far off—very far! I go back to the almond and rose of Damascus!—sleep!"

The room swam before my eyes. I became insensible. When I recovered, I found G—— holding my hand and smiling. He said, "You who have always declared yourself proof against mesmerism have succumbed at last to my friend Richards."

"Where is Mr Richards?"

"Gone, when you passed into a trance—saying quietly to me, 'Your friend will not wake for an hour.'"

I asked, as collectedly as I could, where Mr Richards lodged.

"At the Trafalgar Hotel."

"Give me your arm," said I to G——; "let us call on him; I have something to say."

When we arrived at the hotel, we were told that Mr Richards had returned twenty minutes before, paid his bill, left directions with his servant (a Greek) to pack his effects and proceeded to Malta by the steamer that should leave Southampton the next day. Mr Richards had merely said of his own movements that he had visits to pay in the neighbourhood of London, and it was uncertain whether he should be able to reach Southampton in time for that steamer; if not, he should follow in the next one.

The waiter asked me my name. On my informing him, he gave me a note that Mr Richards had left for me, in case I called.

The note was as follows: "I wished you to utter what was in your mind. You obeyed. I have therefore established power over you. For three months from this day, you can communicate to no living man what has passed between us —you cannot even show this note to the friend by your side. During three months, the silence was complete as to me and mine. Do you doubt my power to lay on you this command?—try to disobey me. At the end of the third month, the spell is raised. For the rest, I spare you. I shall visit your grave a year and a day after it has received you."

So ends this strange story, which I ask no one to believe. I wrote it down exactly three months after I received the above note. I could not write it before, nor could I show to G——, in spite of his urgent request, the note which I read under the gas lamp by his side.

CHILDREN OF THE MOON

by Richard Barham Middleton

The boy stood at the place where the park trees stopped, and the smooth lawns slid away gently to the great house. He was dressed only in a pair of ragged knickerbockers and a gaping buttonless shirt so that his legs and neck, and chest shone silver bare in the moonlight. By day he had a mass of rough golden hair, but now it seemed to brood above his head like a black cloud that made his face deathly white by comparison. On his arms, there lay a great heap of gleaming dew-wet roses and lilies, spoiled of the park flowerbeds. Their cool petals touched his cheek and filled his nostrils with an aching scent. He felt his arms smarting here and there, where the thorns of the roses had torn them in the dark, but these delicate caresses of pain only served to deepen to him the wonder of the night that wrapped him about like a cloak. Behind him, there dreamed the black woods, and over his head, multitudinous stars quivered and balanced in space, but these things were nothing to him, for far across the lawn that was spread knee-deep, with a web of mist there gleamed for his eager eyes the splendour of a fairy palace. Red and orange and gold, the lights of the fairy revels shone from a hundred windows and filled him with wonder that he should see with wakeful eyes the jewels that he had desired so long in sleep. He could only gaze and gaze until his straining eyes filled with tears and set the enchanted lights dancing in the dark. On his ears, that heard no more the crying of the night birds and the quick stir of the rabbits in the brake. There fell the strains of far music. The flowers in his arms seemed to sway to it, and his heartbeat to the deep pulse of the night.

So enraptured were his senses that he did not notice the coming of the girl, and she was able to examine him closely before she called to him softly through the moonlight.

"Boy! Boy!"

At the sound of her voice, he swung around and looked at her with startled eyes. He saw her excited little face and her white dress.

"Are you a fairy?" he asked hoarsely, for the night mist was in his voice.

"No," she said, "I'm a little girl. You're a wood boy, I suppose?"

He stayed silent, regarding her with a puzzled face. Who was this little white creature with the tender voice that had slipped so suddenly out of the night?

"As a matter of fact," the girl continued, "I've come out to have a look at the fairies. There's a ring down in the wood. You can come with me if you like, wood-boy."

He nodded his head silently, for he was afraid to speak to her, and set off through the wood by her side, still clasping the flowers to his breast.

"What were you looking at when I found you?" she asked.

"The palace—the fairy palace," the boy muttered.

"The palace?" the girl repeated. "Why, that's not a palace; that's where I live."

The boy looked at her with new awe; if she were a fairy—— But the girl had noticed that his feet made no sound beside her shoes.

"Don't the thorns prick your feet, wood-boy?" she asked, but the boy said nothing, and they were both silent for a while, the girl looking about her keenly as she walked and the boy watching her face. Presently they came to a wide pool where a little tinkling fountain threw bubbles to the hidden fish.

"Can you swim?" she said to the boy.

He shook his head.

"It's a pity," said the girl; "we might have had a bathe. It would be rather fun in the dark, but it's pretty deep there. We'd better get on to the fairy ring."

The moon had flung queer shadows across the glade in which the ring lay, and when they stood on the edge listening intently, the wood seemed to speak to them with a hundred voices.

"You can take hold of my hand, if you like," said the girl in a whisper.

The boy dropped his flowers about his white feet and felt for the girl's hand in the dark. Soon it lay in his own, a warm live thing that stirred a little with excitement.

"I'm not afraid," the girl said; and so they waited.

* * * * *

The man came upon them suddenly from among the silver birches. He had a knapsack on his back, and his hair was as long as a tramp's. At the sight of him, the girl almost screamed, and her hand trembled in the boys. Some instinct made him hold it tighter.

"What do you want?" he muttered in his hoarse voice.

The man was no less astonished than the children.

"What on earth are you doing here?" he cried. His voice was mild and reassuring, and the girl answered him promptly.

"I came out to look for fairies."

"Oh, that's right enough," commented the man, "and you," he said, turning to the boy, "are you after fairies, too? Oh, I see; picking flowers. Do you mean to sell them?"

The boy shook his head.

"For my sister," he said and stopped abruptly.

"Is your sister fond of flowers?"

"Yes; she's dead."

The man looked at him gravely.

"That's a phrase," he said, "and phrases are the devil. Who told you that dead people like flowers?"

"They always have them," said the boy, blushing at the shame of his pretty thought.

"And what are you looking for?" the girl interrupted.

The man made a mocking grimace and glanced around the glade as if he were afraid of being overheard.

"Dreams," he said bluntly.

The girl pondered this for a moment.

"And your knapsack?" she began.

"Yes," said the man, "it's full of them."

The children looked at the knapsack with interest, the girl's fingers tingling to undo the straps of it.

"What are they like?" she asked.

The man gave a short laugh.

"Very like yours and his, I expect; when you grow older, young woman, you'll find there's really only one dream possible for a sensible person. But you don't want to hear about my troubles. This is more in your line!" He put his hand in his pocket and pulled out a flageolet, which he put to his lips.

"Listen!" he said.

To the girl, it seemed as though the little tune had leapt from the pipe, and was dancing round the ring like a real fairy, while echo came tripping through the trees to join it. The boy gaped and said nothing.

At last, when the fairy was beginning to falter and echo was quite out of breath, the man took the flageolet from his lips.

"Well," he said with a smile.

"Thank you very much," said the girl politely. "I think that was very nice indeed. Oh, boy!" she broke off, "you're hurting my hand!"

The boy's eyes were shining strangely, and he was waving his arms in dismay.

"All the wasted moonlight!" he cried; "the grass is quite wet with it."

The girl turned to him in surprise.

"Why, boy, you've found your voice."

"After that," said the man gravely, as he put his flageolet back in his pocket, "I think I will show you the inside of my knapsack."

The girl bent down eagerly while he loosened the straps but gave a cry of disappointment when she saw the contents.

"Pictures!" she said.

"Pictures," echoed the man drily,—"pictures of dreams. I don't know how you're going to see them. Perhaps the moon will do her best."

The girl looked at them nicely and passed them on one by one to the boy. Presently she made a discovery.

"Oh, boy!" she cried, "your tears are spoiling all the pictures."

"I'm sorry," said the boy huskily; "I can't help it."

"I know," the man said quickly; "it doesn't matter a bit. I expect you've seen these pictures before."

"I know them all," said the boy, "but I have never seen them."

The man frowned.

"It's the devil," he said to himself, "when boys speak English." He turned suddenly to the girl, who was puzzling over the boy's tears. "It's time you went back to bed," he said; "there won't be any fairies tonight. It's too cold for them."

The girl yawned.

"I shall get into a row when I get back if they've found it out. I don't care."

"The moon is fading," said the boy suddenly; "there are no more shadows."

"We will see you through the wood," the man continued, "and say good-night."

He put his pictures back in his knapsack and then walked silently through the murmuring wood. At the edge of the wood, the girl stopped.

"You are a wood boy," she said to the boy, "and you mustn't come any farther. You can give me a kiss if you like."

The boy did not move but stayed beside her awkwardly.

"I think you are a very silly boy," said the girl, with a toss of her head, and she stalked away proudly into the mist.

"Why didn't you kiss her?" asked the man.

"Her lips would burn me," said the boy.

The man and the boy walked slowly across the park.

"Now, boy," said the man, "since civilisation has gone to bed the time has come for you to hear your destiny."

"I am only a poor boy," the boy replied simply. "I don't think I have any destiny."

"Paradox," said the man, "is meant to conceal the insincerity of the aged, not to express the simplicity of youth. But I wander. You have made phrases tonight."

"What are phrases?"

"What are dreams? What are roses? What, in fine, is the moon? Boy, I take you for a moon-child. You hold her pale flowers in your arms, her white beams have caressed your limbs, you prefer the kisses of her cool lips to those of that earth-child; all this is very well. But, above all, you have the music of her great silence; above all, you have her tears. When I played to you on my pipe you recognized the voice of your mother. When I showed you my pictures you recalled the tales with which she hushed you to sleep. And so I knew that you were her son and my little brother."

"The moon has always been my friend," said the boy, "but I did not know that she was my mother."

"Perhaps your sister knows it; the happy dead are glad to seek her for a mother; that is why they are so fond of white flowers."

"We have a mother at home. She works very hard for us."

"But it is your mother among the clouds who makes your life beautiful, and the beauty of your life is the measure of your days."

While the boy reflected on these things, they had reached the gates of the park, and they stole past the silent lodge onto the high road. A man was waiting there in the shadows, and when he saw the boy's companion, he rushed out and seized him by the arm.

"So I've got you," he said; "I don't think I'll let you go again in a hurry."

The son of the moon gave a queer little laugh.

"Why, it's Taylor!" he said pleasantly, "but, Taylor, you know you're making a great mistake."

"Very possibly," said the keeper with a laugh.

"You see this boy here, Taylor; I assure you he is much madder than I am."

Taylor looked at the boy kindly.

"Time you were in bed, Tommy," he said.

"Taylor," said the man earnestly, "this boy has made three phrases. If you don't lock him up he will certainly become a poet. He will set your precious world of sanity ablaze with the fire of his mother, the moon. Your palaces will totter, Taylor, and your kingdoms become as dust. I have warned you."

"That's right, sir; and now you must come with me."

"Boy," said the man generously, "keep your liberty. By grace of Providence, all men in authority are fools. We shall meet again under the light of the moon."

With dreamy eyes, the boy watched the departure of his companion. He had become almost invisible along the road when, miraculously as it seemed, the light of the moon broke through the trees by the wayside and lit up his figure. For a moment, it fell upon his head like a halo and touched the knapsack of dreams with glory. Then all was lost in the blackness of night.

As he turned homeward, the boy felt a cold wind upon his cheek. It was the first breath of dawn.

THE GHOST SHIP

by Richard Barham Middleton

Fairfield is a little village lying near Portsmouth Road, about halfway between London and the sea. Strangers who find it by accident now and then call it a pretty, old-fashioned place; we who live in it and call it home don't find anything very pretty about it, but we should be sorry to live anywhere else. Our minds have taken the shape of the inn and the church and the green, I suppose. At all events, we never feel comfortable out of Fairfield.

Of course, the Cockneys, with their vast houses and noise-ridden streets, can call us rustics if they choose, but for all that, Fairfield is a better place to live than London. The doctor says that when he goes to London, his mind is bruised with the weight of the houses, and he was a Cockney born. He had to live there himself when he was a little chap, but he knows better now. You gentlemen may laugh—perhaps some of you come from London way—but it seems to me that a witness like that is worth a gallon of arguments.

Dull? Well, you might find it dull, but I assure you that I've listened to all the London yarns you have spun tonight, and they're absolutely nothing to the things that happen at Fairfield. It's because of our way of thinking and minding our own business. If one of your Londoners were set down on the green of a Saturday night when the ghosts of the lads who died in the war keep tryst with the lasses who lie in the church-yard, he couldn't help being curious and interfering, and then the ghosts would go somewhere where it was quieter. But we just let them come and go and don't make any fuss, and in consequence, Fairfield is the ghostiest place in all of England. Why I've seen a headless man was sitting on the edge of the well in broad daylight, and the children were playing about his feet as if he were their father. Take my word for it. Spirits know when they are well off as much as human beings.

Still, I must admit that the thing I'm going to tell you about was queer even for our part of the world, where three packs of ghost-hounds regularly hunt during the season, and blacksmith's great-grandfather is busy all night shoeing the dead gentlemen's horses. Now that's a thing that wouldn't happen in London because of their interfering ways, but the blacksmith lies up aloft and sleeps as quietly as a lamb. Once when he had a bad head, he shouted down to them not to make so much noise, and in the morning, he found an old guinea left on the anvil as an apology. He wears it on his watch chain now. But I must get on with my story; if I start telling you about the queer happenings at Fairfield, I'll never stop.

It all came from the great storm in the spring of '97, the year that we had two great storms. This was the first one, and I remember it very well because I found in the morning that it had lifted the thatch of my pigsty into the widow's garden as clean as a boy's kite. When I looked over the hedge, widow—Tom Lamport's widow that was—was prodding for her nasturtiums with a daisy grubber. After I had watched her for a little, I went down to the "Fox and Grapes" to tell the landlord what she had said to me. Landlord, he laughed, being a married man and at ease with the sex. "Come to that," he said, "the tempest has blowed something into my field. A kind of a ship I think it would be."

I was surprised at that until he explained that it was only a ghost ship and would do no hurt to the turnips. We argued that it had been blown up from the sea at Portsmouth, and then we talked of something else. There were two slates down at the parsonage and a big tree in Lumley's meadow. It was a rare storm.

I reckon the wind had blown our ghosts all over England. They were coming back for days afterwards with foundered horses and as footsore as possible, and they were so glad to get back to Fairfield that some of them walked up the street crying like little children. Squire said that his great-grandfather's great-grandfather hadn't looked so dead-beat since the battle of Naseby, and he's an educated man.

What with one thing and another, I should think it was a week before we got straight again, and then one afternoon, I met the landlord on the green, and he had a worried face. "I wish you'd come and have a look at that ship in my field," he said to me; "it seems to me it's leaning real hard on the turnips. I can't bear thinking what the missus will say when she sees it."

I walked down the lane with him, and sure enough, there was a ship in the middle of his field, but such a ship as no man had seen on the water for three hundred years, let alone in the middle of a turnip field. It was all painted black and covered with carvings, and there was a great bay window in the stern for all the world, like the Squire's drawing room. There was a crowd of little black cannons on deck and looking out of her port holes, and she was anchored at each end to the hard ground. I have seen the wonders of the world on picture postcards, but I have never seen anything to equal that.

"She seems very solid for a ghost-ship," I said, seeing the landlord was bothered.

"I should say it's a betwixt and between," he answered, puzzling it over, "but it's going to spoil a matter of fifty turnips, and missus she'll want it moved." We went up to her and touched the side, and it was as hard as a real ship. "Now there's folks in England would call that very curious," he said.

Now I don't know much about ships, but I should think that that ghost ship weighed a solid two hundred tons, and it seemed to me that she had come to stay so that I felt sorry for the landlord, who was a married man. "All the horses in Fairfield won't move her out of my turnips," he said, frowning at her.

Just then, we heard a noise on her deck, and we looked up and saw that a man had come out of her front cabin and was looking down at us very peaceably. He was dressed in a black uniform set out with rusty gold lace, and he had a great cutlass by his side in a brass sheath. "I'm Captain Bartholomew Roberts," he said, in a gentleman's voice, "put in for recruits. I seem to have brought her rather far up the harbour."

"Harbour!" cried the landlord, "why, you're fifty miles from the sea."

Captain Roberts didn't turn a hair. "So much as that, is it?" he said coolly. "Well, it's of no consequence."

The landlord was a bit upset at this. "I don't want to be unneighbourly," he said, "but I wish you hadn't brought your ship into my field. You see, my wife sets great store on these turnips."

The captain took a pinch of snuff out of a fine gold box that he pulled out of his pocket and dusted his fingers with a silk handkerchief in a very genteel fashion. "I'm only here for a few months," he said, "but if a testimony of my esteem would pacify your good lady, I should be content," and with the words, he loosed a great gold brooch from the neck of his coat and tossed it down to landlord.

The landlord blushed as red as a strawberry. "I'm not denying she's fond of jewellery," he said, "but it's too much for half a sackful of turnips." And indeed, it was a handsome brooch.

The captain laughed. "Tut, man," he said, "it's a forced sale, and you deserve a good price. Say no more about it;" nodding good day to us, he turned on his heel and went into the cabin. The landlord walked back up the lane like a man with a weight off his mind. "That tempest has blown me a bit of luck," he said; "the missus will be much pleased with that brooch. It's better than blacksmith's guinea, any day."

Ninety-seven was Jubilee year, the year of the second Jubilee, you remember, and we had great doings at Fairfield so that we hadn't much time to bother about the ghost-ship through anyhow it isn't our way to meddle in things that don't concern us. The landlord saw his tenant once or twice when he was hoeing his turnips and passed the time of day, and the landlord's wife wore her new brooch to church every Sunday. But we didn't mix much with the ghosts at any time, all except an idiot lad there was in the village, and he didn't know the difference between a man and a ghost, poor innocent! On Jubilee Day, however, somebody told Captain Roberts why the church bells were ringing, and he hoisted a flag and fired off his guns like a loyal Englishman. 'Tis true the guns were shotted, and one of the round shots knocked a hole in Farmer Johnstone's barn, but nobody thought much of that in such a season of rejoicing.

It wasn't till our celebrations were over that we noticed that anything was wrong in Fairfield. 'Twas shoemaker who told me first about it one morning at the "Fox and Grapes." "You know my great great-uncle?" he said to me.

"You mean Joshua, the quiet lad," I answered, knowing him well.

"Quiet!" said the shoemaker indignantly. "Quiet, you call him, coming home at three o'clock every morning as drunk as a magistrate and waking up the whole house with his noise."

"Why, it can't be Joshua!" I said for I knew him as one of the most respectable young ghosts in the village.

"Joshua it is," said the shoemaker, "and one of these nights, he'll find himself out in the street if he isn't careful."

This kind of talk shocked me, I can tell you, for I don't like to hear a man abusing his own family, and I could hardly believe that a steady youngster like Joshua had taken to drink. But just then, in came butcher Aylwin in such a temper that he could hardly drink his beer. "The young puppy! the young puppy!" he kept on saying, and it was sometime before the shoemaker, and I found out that he was talking about his ancestor that fell at Senlac.

"Drink?" said the shoemaker hopefully, for we all like the company in our misfortunes, and the butcher nodded grimly.

"The young noodle," he said, emptying his tankard.

After that, I kept my ears open, and it was the same story all over the village. There was hardly a young man among all the ghosts of Fairfield who didn't roll home in the small hours of the morning the worse for liquor. I used to wake up at night and hear them stumble past my house, singing outrageous songs. The worst of it was that we couldn't keep the scandal to ourselves, and the folk at Greenhill began to talk of "sodden Fairfield" and taught their children to sing a song about us:

"Sodden Fairfield, sodden Fairfield, has no use for bread-and-butter, Rum for breakfast, rum for dinner, rum for tea, and rum for supper!"

We are easy-going in our village, but we didn't like that.

Of course, we soon found out where the young fellows went to get the drink, and the landlord was terribly cut up that his tenant should have turned out so badly, but his wife wouldn't hear of parting with the brooch so that he couldn't give the Captain notice to quit. But as time went on, things grew from bad to worse, and at all hours of the day, you would see those young reprobates sleeping it off on the village green. Nearly every afternoon, a ghost wagon used to jolt down to the ship with a lading of rum, and though the older ghosts seemed inclined to give the Captain's hospitality the go-by, the youngsters were neither to hold nor to bind.

So one afternoon, when I was taking my nap, I heard a knock at the door, and there was a parson looking very serious, like a man with a job before him that he didn't altogether relish. "I'm going down to talk to the Captain about all this drunkenness in the village, and I want you to come with me," he said straight out.

I can't say that I fancied the visit much, myself, and I tried to hint to parson that as, after all, they were only a lot of ghosts, it didn't very much matter.

"Dead or alive, I'm responsible for the good conduct," he said, "and I'm going to do my duty and put a stop to this continued disorder. And you are coming with me, John Simmons." So I went, parson being a persuasive kind of man. We went down to the ship, and as we approached her, I could see the Captain tasting the air on deck. When he saw parson he took off his hat very politely, and I can tell you that I was relieved to find that he had a proper respect for the cloth. Parson acknowledged his salute and spoke out stoutly enough. "Sir, I should be glad to have a word with you."

"Come on board, sir; come on board," said the Captain, and I could tell by his voice that he knew why we were there. Parson and I climbed up an uneasy kind of ladder, and the Captain took us into the great cabin at the back of the ship, where the bay window was. It was the most wonderful place you ever saw in your life, all full of gold and silver plate, swords with jewelled scabbards, carved oak chairs, and great chests that looked as though they were bursting with guineas. Even parson was surprised, and he did not shake his head very hard when the Captain took down some silver cups and poured us out a drink of rum. I tasted mine, and I don't mind saying that it changed my view of things entirely. There was nothing betwixt and between about that rum, and I felt that it was ridiculous to blame the lads for drinking too much of stuff like that. It seemed to fill my veins with honey and fire.

Parson put the case squarely to the Captain, but I didn't listen much to what he said; I was busy sipping my drink and looking through the window at the fishes swimming to and fro over the landlord's turnips. Just then, it seemed the most natural thing in the world that they should be there, though afterwards, of course, I could see that that proved it was a ghost ship.

But even then, I thought it was queer when I saw a drowned sailor float by in the thin air with his hair and beard all full of bubbles. It was the first time I had seen anything quite like that at Fairfield.

All the time I was regarding the wonders of the deep parson was telling Captain Roberts how there was no peace or rest in the village owing to the curse of drunkenness and what a bad example the youngsters were setting to the older ghosts. The Captain listened very attentively and only put in a word now and then about boys being boys and young men sowing their wild oats. But when parson had finished his speech, he filled up our silver cups and said to parson, with a flourish, "I should be sorry to cause trouble anywhere where I have been made welcome, and you will be glad to hear that I put to sea tomorrow night. And now you must drink me a prosperous voyage." So we all stood up and drank the toast with honour, and that noble rum was like hot oil in my veins.

After that, Captain showed us some of the curiosities he had brought back from foreign parts, and we were greatly amazed, though afterwards, I couldn't clearly remember what they were. And then I found myself walking across the turnips with parson, and I was telling him of the glories of the deep that I had seen through the window of the ship. He turned on me severely. "If I were you, John Simmons," he said, "I should go straight home to bed." He has a way of putting things that wouldn't occur to an ordinary man, has parson, and I did as he told me.

Well, the next day, it came on to blow, and it blew harder and harder till about eight o'clock at night. I heard a noise and looked out into the garden. I dare say you won't believe me, it seems a bit tall even to me, but the wind had lifted the thatch of my pigsty into the widow's garden a second time. I thought I wouldn't wait to hear what the widow had to say about it, so I went across the green to the "Fox and Grapes", and the wind was so strong that I danced along on tiptoe like a girl at the fair. When I got to the inn landlord had to help me shut the door; it seemed as though a dozen goats were pushing against it to come in out of the storm.

"It's a powerful tempest," he said, drawing the beer. "I hear there's a chimney down at Dickory End."

"It's a funny thing how these sailors know about the weather," I answered. "When Captain said he was going tonight, I was thinking it would take a capful of wind to carry the ship back to sea, but now here's more than a capful."

"Ah, yes," said the landlord, "it's tonight he goes true enough, and, mind you, though he treated me handsome over the rent, I'm not sure it's a loss to the village. I don't hold with gentrice who fetch their drink from London instead of helping local traders to get their living."

"But you haven't got any rum like his," I said to draw him out.

His neck grew red above his collar, and I was afraid I'd gone too far, but after a while, he got his breath with a grunt.

"John Simmons," he said, "if you've come down here this windy night to talk a lot of fool's talk, you've wasted a journey."

Well, of course, then I had to smooth him down by praising his rum, and Heaven forgives me for swearing it was better than Captains. For the like of that rum, no living lips have tasted save mine and parson's. But somehow or other, I brought the landlord round, and presently we must have a glass of his best to prove its quality.

"Beat that if you can!" he cried, and we both raised our glasses to our mouths, only to stop halfway and look at each other in amazement. For the wind that had been howling outside like an outrageous dog had all of a sudden turned as melodious as the carol-boys of a Christmas Eve.

"Surely that's not my Martha," whispered the landlord, Martha being his great-aunt that lived in the loft overhead.

We went to the door, and the wind burst it open so that the handle was driven clean into the plaster of the wall. But we didn't think about that at the time; for over our heads, sailing very comfortably through the windy stars, was the ship that had passed the summer in the landlord's field. Her portholes and her bay window were blazing with lights, and there was a noise of singing and fiddling on her decks. "He's gone," shouted the landlord above the storm, "and he's taken half the village with him!" I could only nod in answer, not having lungs like bellows of leather.

In the morning, we were able to measure the strength of the storm, and over and above my pigsty, there was enough damage wrought in the village to keep us busy. True it is that the children had to break down no branches for the firing that autumn since the wind had strewn the woods with more than they could carry away. Many of our ghosts were scattered abroad, but this time very few came back, all the young men having sailed with Captain, and not only ghosts, for a poor half-witted lad was missing, and we reckoned that he had stowed himself away or perhaps shipped as cabin-boy, not knowing any better.

What with the lamentations of the ghost girls and the grumbling of families who had lost an ancestor, the village was upset for a while, and the funny thing was that it was the folk who had complained most of the carryings-on of the youngsters who made most noise now that they were gone. I hadn't any sympathy with shoemaker or butcher, who ran about saying how much they missed their lads, but it made me grieve to hear the poor bereaved girls calling their lovers by name on the village green at nightfall. It didn't seem fair to me that they should have lost their men a second time, after giving up life in order to join them, as like as not. Still, not even a spirit can be sorry forever, and after a few months, we made up our minds that the folk who had sailed in the ship were never coming back, and we didn't talk about it anymore.

And then one day, I dare say it would be a couple of years after, when the whole business was quite forgotten, who should come trapesing along the road from Portsmouth but the daft lad who had gone away with the ship, without waiting till he was dead to become a ghost. You never saw such a boy as that in all your life. He had a great rusty cutlass hanging to a string at his waist, and he was tattooed all over in fine colors so that even his face looked like a girl's sampler. He had a handkerchief in his hand full of foreign shells and old-fashioned pieces of small money, very curious, and he walked up to the well outside his mother's house and drew himself a drink as if he had been nowhere in particular.

The worst of it was that he had come back as soft-headed as he went, and try as we might, we couldn't get anything reasonable out of him. He talked a lot of gibberish about keel-hauling and walking the plank and crimson murders—things which a decent sailor should know nothing about, so that it seemed to me that for all his manners, Captain had been more of a pirate than a gentleman mariner. But to draw sense out of that boy was as hard as picking cherries off a crab tree. One silly tale he had that he kept on drifting back to, and to hear him, you would have thought that it was the only thing that happened to him in his life. "We was at anchor," he would say, "off an island called the Basket of Flowers, and the sailors had caught a lot of parrots and we were teaching them to swear. Up and down the decks, up and down the decks, and the language they used was dreadful. Then we looked up and saw the masts of the Spanish ship outside the harbour. Outside the harbour they were, so we threw the parrots into the sea and sailed out to fight. And all the parrots were drownded in the sea and the language they used was dreadful." That's the sort of boy he was, nothing but silly talk of parrots when we asked him about the fighting. And we never had a chance of teaching him better, for two days after he ran away again, and hasn't been seen since.

That's my story, and I assure you that things like that are happening at Fairfield all the time. The ship has never come back, but somehow as people grow older, they seem to think that on one of these windy nights, she'll come sailing in over the hedges with all the lost ghosts on board. Well, when she comes, she'll be welcome. There's one ghost-lass that has never grown tired of waiting for her lad to return. Every night you'll see her out on the green, straining her poor eyes with looking for the mast lights among the stars. A faithful lass you'd call her, and I think you'd be right.

Landlord's field wasn't a penny the worse for the visit, but they do say that since then, the turnips that have been grown in it have tasted of rum.

THE EBONY FRAME

by Edith Nesbit

To be rich is a luxurious sensation—the more so when you have plumbed the depths of hard-up-ness as a Fleet Street hack, a picker-up of unconsidered pars, a reporter, an unappreciated journalist—all callings utterly inconsistent with one's family feeling and one's direct descent from the Dukes of Picardy.

When my Aunt Dorcas died and left me seven hundred a year and a furnished house in Chelsea, I felt that life had nothing left to offer except immediate possession of the legacy. Even Mildred Mayhew, whom I had hitherto regarded as my life's light, became less luminous. I was not engaged to Mildred, but I lodged with her mother, and I sang duets with Mildred and gave her gloves when it would run to it, which was seldom. She was a dear good girl, and I meant to marry her someday. It is very nice to feel that a good little woman is thinking of you—it helps you in your work—and it is pleasant to know she will say "Yes" when you say "Will you?"

But, as I say, my legacy almost put Mildred out of my head, especially as she was staying with friends in the country just then.

Before the first gloss was off my new mourning I was seated in my aunt's own armchair in front of the fire in the dining room of my own house. My own house! It was grand but rather lonely. I did think of Mildred just then.

The room was comfortably furnished with oak and leather. On the walls hung a few fairly good oil paintings, but the space above the mantelpiece was disfigured by an exceedingly bad print, "The Trial of Lord William Russell," framed in a dark frame. I got up to look at it. I had visited my aunt with dutiful regularity, but I never remembered seeing this frame before. It was not intended for a print but for an oil painting. It was of fine ebony, beautifully and curiously carved.

I looked at it with growing interest, and when my aunt's housemaid—I had retained her modest staff of servants—came in with the lamp, I asked her how long the print had been there.

"Mistress only bought it two days afore she was took ill," she said, "but the frame—she didn't want to buy a new one—so she got this out of the attic. There's lots of curious old things there, sir."

"Had my aunt had this frame long?"

"Oh yes, sir. It come long afore I did, and I've been here seven years come Christmas. There was a picture in it —that's upstairs too—but it's that black and ugly it might as well be a chimley-back."

I felt the desire to see this picture. What if it were some priceless old master in which my aunt's eyes had only seen rubbish?

Directly after breakfast the next morning, I paid a visit to the lumber room.

It was crammed with old furniture enough to stock a curiosity shop. All the house was furnished solidly in the early Victorian style, and in this room, everything not in keeping with the "drawing-room suite" ideal was stowed away. Tables of papier maché and mother-of-pearl, straight-backed chairs with twisted feet and faded needlework cushions, firescreens of old-world design, oak bureaux with brass handles, a little work table with its faded moth-eaten silk flutings hanging in disconsolate shreds: on these and the dust that covered them blazed the full daylight as I drew up the blinds. I promised myself a good time in re-enshrining these household gods in my parlour and promoting the Victorian suite to the attic. But at present, my business was to find the picture as "black as the chimley-back;" and presently, behind a heap of hideous still-life studies, I found it.

Jane, the housemaid, identified it at once. I took it downstairs carefully and examined it. No subject and no color were distinguishable. There was a splodge of a darker tint in the middle, but whether it was a figure or tree or house, no man could have told. It seemed to be painted on a very thick panel bound with leather. I decided to send it to one of those persons who pour on rotting family portraits the water of eternal youth—mere soap and water Mr Besant tells us it is, but even as I did so, the thought occurred to me to try my own restorative hand at a corner of it.

My bath sponge, soap, and nailbrush vigorously applied for a few seconds showed me that there was no picture to clean! Bare oak presented itself to my persevering brush. I tried the other side, Jane watching me with indulgent interest. The same result. Then the truth dawned on me. Why was the panel so thick? I tore off the leather binding, and the panel divided and fell to the ground in a cloud of dust. There were two pictures—they had been nailed face to face. I leaned them against the wall, and the next moment I was leaning against it myself.

One of the pictures was me—a perfect portrait—no shade of expression or turn of feature wanting. Myself—in a cavalier dress, "love-locks and all!" When had this been done? And how, without my knowledge? Was this some whim of my aunt's?

"Lor', sir!" the shrill surprise of Jane at my elbow; "what a lovely photo it is! Was it a fancy ball, sir?"

"Yes," I stammered. "I—I don't think I want anything more now. You can go."

She went, and I turned, still with my heart beating violently, to the other picture. This was a woman of the type of beauty beloved by Burne Jones and Rossetti—straight nose, low brows, full lips, thin hands, large deep luminous eyes. She wore a black velvet gown. It was a full-length portrait. Her arms rested on a table beside her, and her head on her hands, but her face was turned full forward, and her eyes met those of the spectator bewilderingly. On the table by her were compasses and instruments whose uses I did not know, books, a goblet, and a miscellaneous heap of papers and pens. I saw all this afterwards. I believe it was a quarter of an hour before I could turn my eyes away from hers. I have never seen any other eyes like hers. They appealed, as a child's or a dog's do; they commanded, as might those of an empress.

"Shall I sweep up the dust, sir?" Curiosity had brought Jane back. I acceded. I turned from her my portrait. I kept between her and the woman in the black velvet. When I was alone again, I tore down "The Trial of Lord William Russell," and I put the picture of the woman in its strong ebony frame.

Then I wrote to a frame-maker for a frame for my portrait. It had so long lived face to face with this beautiful witch that I had not the heart to banish it from her presence, from which it will be perceived that I am by nature a somewhat sentimental person.

The new frame came home, and I hung it opposite the fireplace. An exhaustive search among my aunt's papers showed no explanation of the portrait of myself, no history of the portrait of the woman with the wonderful eyes. I only learned that all the old furniture together had come to my aunt at the death of my great-uncle, the head of the family; and I should have concluded that the resemblance was only a family one if everyone who came in had not exclaimed at the "speaking likeness." I adopted Jane's "fancy ball" explanation.

And there, one might suppose, the matter of the portraits ended. One might suppose it, that is, if there were not evidently a good deal more written here about it. However, to me, then, the matter seemed to have ended.

I went to see Mildred; I invited her and her mother to come and stay with me. I rather avoided glancing at the picture in the ebony frame. I could not forget, nor remember without singular emotion, the look in the eyes of that woman when mine first met them. I shrank from meeting that look again.

I reorganized the house somewhat, preparing for Mildred's visit. I turned the dining room into a drawing room. I brought down much of the old-fashioned furniture, and, after a long day of arranging and re-arranging, I sat down before the fire, and, lying back in a pleasant languor, I idly raised my eyes to the picture. I met her dark, deep hazel eyes, and once more, my gaze was held fixed as by a strong magic—the kind of fascination that keeps one sometimes staring for whole minutes into one's own eyes in the glass. I gazed into her eyes and felt my own dilate, pricked with a smart like the smart of tears.

"I wish," I said, "oh, how I wish you were a woman, and not a picture! Come down! Ah, come down!"

I laughed at myself as I spoke, but even as I laughed, I held out my arms.

I was not sleepy; I was not drunk. I was as wide awake and as sober as ever was a man in this world. And yet, as I held out my arms, I saw the eyes of the picture dilate, her lips tremble—if I were to be hanged for saying it, it is true. Her hands moved slightly, and a sort of flicker of a smile passed over her face.

I sprang to my feet. "This won't do," I said, still aloud. "Firelight does play strange tricks. I'll have the lamp."

I pulled myself together and made for the bell. My hand was on it when I heard a sound behind me and turned—the bell still unrung. The fire had burned low, and the corners of the room were deeply shadowed, but surely, there—behind the tall worked chair—was something darker than a shadow.

"I must face this out," I said, "or I shall never be able to face myself again." I left the bell, seized the poker and battered the dull coals to a blaze. Then I stepped back resolutely and looked up at the picture. The ebony frame was empty! From the shadow of the worked chair came a silken rustle, and out of the shadow, the woman of the picture was coming—coming towards me.

I hope I shall never again know a moment of terror so blank and absolute. I could not have moved or spoken to save my life. Either all the known laws of nature were nothing, or I was mad. I stood trembling, but, I am thankful to remember, I stood still while the black velvet gown swept across the hearthrug towards me.

The next moment a hand touched me—a hand soft, warm, and human—and a low voice said, "You called me. I am here."

At that touch and that voice, the world seemed to give a sort of bewildering half-turn. I hardly know how to express it, but at once, it seemed not awful—not even unusual—for portraits to become flesh—only most natural, most right, most unspeakably fortunate.

I laid my hand on hers. I looked from her to my portrait. I could not see it in the firelight.

"We are not strangers," I said.

"Oh no, not strangers." Those luminous eyes were looking up into mine—those red lips were near me. With a passionate cry—a sense of having suddenly recovered life's one great good that had seemed wholly lost—I clasped her in my arms. She was no ghost—she was a woman—the only woman in the world.

"How long," I said, "O love—how long since I lost you?"

She leaned back, hanging her full weight on the hands that were clasped behind my head.

"How can I tell how long? There is no time in hell," she answered.

It was not a dream. Ah, no—there are no such dreams. I wish to God there could be. When in dreams do I see her eyes, hear her voice, feel her lips against my cheek, hold her hands to my lips, as I did that night—the supreme night of my life? At first, we hardly spoke. It seemed enough—

"... after long grief and pain,

To feel the arms of my true love

Round me once again."

It is very difficult to tell this story. There are no words to express the sense of glad reunion, the complete realization of every hope and dream of a life that came upon me as I sat with my hand in hers and looked into her eyes.

How could it have been a dream when I left her sitting in the straight-backed chair and went down to the kitchen to tell the maids I should want nothing more—that I was busy and did not wish to be disturbed; when I fetched wood for the fire with my own hands, and, bringing it in, found her still sitting there—saw the little brown head turn as I entered, saw the love in her dear eyes; when I threw myself at her feet and blessed the day I was born since life had given me this?

Not a thought of Mildred: all the other things in my life were a dream—this, its one splendid reality.

"I am wondering," she said after a while when we had made such cheer each of the other as true lovers may after long parting—"I am wondering how much you remember of our past."

"I remember nothing," I said. "Oh, my dear lady, my dear sweetheart—I remember nothing but that I love you—that I have loved you all my life."

"You remember nothing—really nothing?"

"Only that I am yours; that we have both suffered; that——Tell me, my mistress dear, all that you remember. Explain it all to me. Make me understand. And yet——No, I don't want to understand. It is enough that we are together."

If it was a dream, why have I never dreamed it again?

She leaned down towards me, her arm lay on my neck, and drew my head till it rested on her shoulder. "I am a ghost, I suppose," she said, laughing softly, and her laughter stirred memories which I just grasped at and just missed. "But you and I know better, don't we? I will tell you everything you have forgotten. We loved each other— ah! no, you have not forgotten that—and when you came back from the war we were to be married. Our pictures were painted before you went away. You know I was more learned than women of that day. Dear one, when you were gone they said I was a witch. They tried me. They said I should be burned. Just because I had looked at the stars and had gained more knowledge than they, they must needs bind me to a stake and let me be eaten by the fire. And you far away!"

Her whole body trembled and shrank. O love, what dream would have told me that my kisses would soothe even that memory?

"The night before," she went on, "the devil did come to me. I was innocent before—you know it, don't you? And even then my sin was for you—for you—because of the exceeding love I bore you. The devil came, and I sold my soul to the eternal flame. But I got a good price. I got the right to come back through my picture (if anyone looking at it wished for me), as long as my picture stayed in its ebony frame. That frame was not carved by man's hand. I got the right to come back to you. Oh, my heart's heart, and another thing I won, which you shall hear anon. They burned me for a witch. They made me suffer hell on earth. Those faces, all crowding round, the crackling wood and the smell of the smoke——"

"O love! no more—no more."

"When my mother sat that night before my picture, she wept and cried, 'Come back, my poor lost child!' And I went to her with glad leaps of heart. Dear, she shrank from me, she fled, she shrieked and moaned of ghosts. She had our pictures covered from sight and put them again in the ebony frame. She had promised me my picture should always stay there. Ah, through all these years, your face was against mine."

She paused.

"But the man you loved?"

"You came home. My picture was gone. They lied to you, and you married another woman, but someday I knew you would walk the world again and that I should find you."

"The other gain?" I asked.

"The other gain," she said slowly, "I gave my soul for. It is this. If you also will give up your hopes of heaven I can remain a woman, I can move in your world—I can be your wife. Oh, my dear, after all these years, at last—at last."

"If I sacrifice my soul," I said slowly, with no thought of the imbecility of such talk in our "so-called nineteenth century"—"if I sacrifice my soul, I win you? Why, love, it's a contradiction in terms. You are my soul."

Her eyes looked straight into mine. Whatever might happen, whatever did happen, whatever may happen, our two souls at that moment met and became one.

"Then you choose—you deliberately choose—to give up your hopes of heaven for me, as I gave up mine for you?"

"I decline," I said, "to give up my hope of heaven on any terms. Tell me what I must do, that you and I may make our heaven here—as now, my dear love."

"I will tell you tomorrow," she said. "Be alone here tomorrow night—twelve is ghost's time, isn't it?—and then I will come out of the picture and never go back to it. I shall live with you, and die, and be buried, and there will be an end of me. But we shall live first, my heart's heart."

I laid my head on her knee. A strange drowsiness overcame me. Holding her hand against my cheek, I lost consciousness. When I awoke, the grey November dawn was glimmering, ghost-like, through the uncurtained window. My head was pillowed on my arm, which rested —I raised my head quickly—ah! not on my lady's knee but on the needle-worked cushion of the straight-backed chair. I sprang to my feet. I was stiff with cold and dazed with dreams, but I turned my eyes to the picture. There she sat, my lady, my dear love. I held out my arms, but the passionate cry I would have uttered died on my lips. She had said twelve o'clock. Her lightest word was my law. So I only stood in front of the picture and gazed into those grey-green eyes till tears of passionate happiness filled my own.

"Oh, my dear, my dear, how shall I pass the hours till I hold you again?"

No thought, then, of my whole life's completion and consummation being a dream.

I staggered up to my room, fell across my bed, and slept heavily and dreamlessly. When I awoke, it was high noon. Mildred and her mother were coming to lunch.

I remembered, at one shock, Mildred's coming and her existence.

Now, indeed, the dream began.

With a penetrating sense of the futility of any action apart from her, I gave the necessary orders for the reception of my guests. When Mildred and her mother came, I received them with cordiality, but my genial phrases all seemed to be someone else's. My voice sounded like an echo; my heart was otherwhere.

Still, the situation was not intolerable until the hour when afternoon tea was served in the drawing room. Mildred and her mother kept the conversational pot boiling with a profusion of genteel commonplaces, and I bore it, as one can bear mild purgatories when one is in sight of heaven. I looked up at my sweetheart in the ebony frame, and I felt that anything that might happen, any irresponsible imbecility, any bathos of boredom, was nothing if, after it all, she came to me again.

And yet, when Mildred, too, looked at the portrait and said, "What a fine lady! One of your flames, Mr Devigne?" I had a sickening sense of impotent irritation, which became absolute torture when Mildred—how could I ever have admired that chocolate-box barmaid style of prettiness?—threw herself into the high-backed chair, covering the needlework with her ridiculous flounces, and added, "Silence gives consent! Who is it, Mr Devigne? Tell us all about her: I am sure she has a story."

Poor little Mildred, sitting there smiling, serene in her confidence that her every word charmed me—sitting there with her rather pinched waist, her rather tight boots, her rather vulgar voice—sitting in the chair where my dear lady had sat when she told me her story! I could not bear it.

"Don't sit there," I said; "it's not comfortable!"

But the girl would not be warned. With a laugh that set every nerve in my body vibrating with annoyance, she said, "Oh, dear! mustn't I even sit in the same chair as your black-velvet woman?"

I looked at the chair in the picture. It was the same, and in her chair, Mildred was sitting. Then a horrible sense of the reality of Mildred came upon me. Was all this a reality after all? But for a fortunate chance, might Mildred have occupied not only her chair but her place in my life? I rose.

"I hope you won't think me very rude," I said, "but I am obliged to go out."

I forget what appointment I alleged. The lie came readily enough.

I faced Mildred's pouts with the hope that she and her mother would not wait for dinner for me. I fled. In another minute, I was safe, alone, under the chill, cloudy autumn sky—free to think, think, think of my dear lady.

I walked for hours along streets and squares; I lived over, again and again, every look, word, and hand touch— every kiss; I was completely, unspeakably happy.

Mildred has utterly forgotten. My lady of the ebony frame filled my heart and soul, and spirit.

As I heard eleven booms through the fog, I turned and went home.

When I got to my street, I found a crowd surging through it, a strong red light filling the air.

A house was on fire. Mine.

I elbowed my way through the crowd.

The picture of my lady—that, at least, I could save!

As I sprang up the steps, I saw, as in a dream—yes, all this was really dream-like—I saw Mildred leaning out of the first-floor window, wringing her hands.

"Come back, sir," cried a fireman; "we'll get the young lady out right enough."

But my lady? I went on up the stairs, cracking, smoking, and as hot as hell, to the room where her picture was. Strange to say, I only felt that the picture was a thing we should like to look on through the long glad wedded life that was to be ours. I never thought of it as being one with her.

As I reached the first floor, I felt arms around my neck. The smoke was too thick for me to distinguish features.

"Save me!" a voice whispered. I clasped a figure in my arms and, with a strange dis-ease, bore it down the shaking stairs and out into safety. It was Mildred. I knew that directly I clasped her.

"Stand back," cried the crowd.

"Every one's safe," cried a fireman.

The flames leapt from every window. The sky grew redder and redder. I sprang from the hands that would have held me. I leapt up the steps. I crawled up the stairs. Suddenly the whole horror of the situation came to me. "As long as my picture remains in the ebony frame." What if the picture and frame perished together?

I fought with the fire and with my own choking inability to fight with it. I pushed on. I must save my picture. I reached the drawing room.

As I sprang in, I saw my lady—I swear it—through the smoke and the flames, hold out her arms to me—to me —who came too late to save her and to save my own life's joy. I never saw her again.

Before I could reach her or cry out to her, I felt the floor yield beneath my feet, and I fell into the fiery hell below.

How did they save me? What does that matter? They saved me somehow—curse them. Every stick of my aunt's furniture was destroyed. My friends pointed out that, as the furniture was heavily insured, the carelessness of a nightly-studious housemaid had done me no harm.

No harm!

That was how I won and lost my only love.

I deny, with all my soul in denial, that it was a dream. There are no such dreams. Dreams of longing and pain there are in plenty, but dreams of complete, of unspeakable happiness—ah, no—it is the rest of life that is the dream.

But if I think that, why have I married Mildred and grown stout and dull and prosperous?

I tell you it is all this that is the dream; my dear lady, only is the reality. And what does it matter what one does in a dream?

WHEN I WAS DEAD

by Vincent O'Sullivan

"And yet my heart

Will not confess he owes the malady

That doth my life besiege."

– All's Well That Ends Well

That was the worst of Ravenel Hall. The passages were long and gloomy, the rooms were musty and dull, and even the pictures were sombre and their subjects dire. On an autumn evening, when the wind soughed and ailed through the trees in the park, and the dead leaves whistled and chattered while the rain clamoured at the windows, its small wonder that folks with gentle nerves went a-straying in their wits! An acute nervous system is a grievous burthen on the deck of a yacht under sunlit skies: at Ravenel, the chain of nerves was prone to clash and jangle a funeral march. Nerves must be pampered in a tea-drinking community; and the ghost that your grandfather, with a skinful of port, could face and never tremble, sets you, in your sobriety, sweating and shivering; or, becoming scared (poor ghost!) of your bulged eyes and dropping jaw, he quenches expectation by not appearing at all. So I am left to conclude that it was tea which made my acquaintance afraid to stay at Ravenel. Even Wilvern gave over, and as he is in the Guards and a polo player, his nerves ought to be strong enough. On the night before he went, I was explaining to him my theory, that if you place some drops of human blood near you, and then concentrate your thoughts, you will after a while see before you a man or a woman who will stay with you during long hours of the night, and even meet you at unexpected places during the day. I was explaining this theory, I repeat, when he interrupted me with words, senseless enough, which sent me fencing and parrying strangers —on my guard.

"I say, Alistair, my dear chap!" he began, "you ought to get out of this place and go up to Town and knock about a bit—you really ought, you know."

"Yes," I replied, "and get poisoned at the hotels by bad food and at the clubs by bad talk, I suppose. No, thank you: and let me say that your care for my health enervates me."

"Well, you can do as you like," says he, rapping with his feet on the floor. "I'm hanged if I stay here after to-morrow I'll be staring mad if I do!"

He was my last visit. Some weeks after his departure, I was sitting in the library with my drops of blood by me. I had gotten my theory nearly perfect by this time, but there was one difficulty. The figure which I had ever before me was the figure of an old woman with her hair divided in the middle, and her hair fell to her shoulders, white on one side and black on the other. She was a complete old woman, but, alas! she was eyeless, and when I tried to construct the eyes, she would shrivel and rot in my sight. But tonight I was thinking, thinking, as I had never thought before, and my eyes were just creeping into my head when I heard a terrible crash outside as if some heavy substance had fallen. Of a sudden, the door was flung open, and two maid-servants entered. They glanced at the rug under my chair, and at that, they turned a sick white, cried on God, and huddled out.

"How dare you enter the library in this manner?" I demanded sternly. No answer came back from them, so I started in pursuit. I found all the servants in the house gathered in a knot at the end of the passage.

"Mrs Pebble," I said smartly to the housekeeper, "I want those two women discharged to-morrow. It's an outrage! You ought to be more careful." But she was not attending to me. Her face was distorted with terror.

"Ah dear, ah dear!" she went. "We had better all go to the library together," says she to the others.

"Am I master of my own house, Mrs Pebble?" I inquired, bringing my knuckles down with a bang on the table.

None of them seemed to see me or hear me: I might as well have been shrieking in a desert. I followed them down the passage and forbade them to enter the library.

But they trooped past me and stood with a clutter round the hearth rug. Then three or four of them began dragging and lifting, as if they were lifting a helpless body, and stumbled with their imaginary burthen over to a sofa. Old Soames, the butler, stood near.

"Poor young gentleman!" he said with a sob. "I've knowed him since he was a baby. And to think of him being dead like this and so young, too!"

I crossed the room. "What's all this, Soames!" I cried, shaking him roughly by the shoulders. "I'm not dead. I'm here—here!" As he did not stir, I got a little scared. "Soames, old friend!" I called, "don't you know me! Don't you know the little boy you used to play with? Say I'm not dead, Soames, please, Soames!"

He stooped down and kissed the sofa. "I think one of the men ought to ride over to the village for the doctor, Mr Soames," says Mrs Pebble, and he shuffled out to give the order.

Now, this doctor was an ignorant dog whom I had been forced to exclude from the house because he went about proclaiming his belief in a saving God at the same time that he proclaimed himself a man of science. He, I was resolved, should never cross my threshold, and I followed Mrs Pebble through the house, screaming out prohibition. But I did not catch even a groan from her, not a nod of the head, nor a cast of the eye, to show that she had heard.

I met the doctor at the door of the library. "Well," I sneered, throwing my hand in his face, "have you come to teach me some new prayers?"

He brushed by me as if he had not felt the blow, and knelt down by the sofa.

"Rupture of a vessel on the brain, I think," he says to Soames and Mrs Pebble after a short moment. "He has been dead some hours. Poor fellow! You had better telegraph for his sister, and I will send up the undertaker to arrange the body."

"You liar!" I yelled. "You whining liar! How have you the insolence to tell my servants that I am dead, when you see me here face to face?"

He was far in the passage, with Soames and Mrs Pebble at his heels, ere I had ended, and not one of the three turned round.

All that night, I sat in the library. Strangely enough, I had no wish to sleep, nor during the time that followed had I any craving to eat. In the morning, the men came, and although I ordered them out, they proceeded to minister about something I could not see. So all day I stayed in the library or wandered about the house, and at night the men came again bringing with them a coffin. Then, in my humour, thinking it a shame that so fine a coffin should be empty, I lay the night in it and slept a soft dreamless sleep—the softest sleep I have ever slept. And when the men came the next day, I rested still, and the undertaker shaved me. A strange valet!

In the evening after that, I was coming downstairs when I noted some luggage in the hall, and so learned that my sister had arrived. I had not seen this woman since her marriage, and I loathed her more than I loathed any creature in this ill-organized world. She was very beautiful, I think—tall, dark, and straight as a ramrod—and she had an unruly passion for scandal and dress. I suppose the reason I disliked her so intensely was, that she had a habit of making one aware of her presence when she was several yards off. At half-past nine o'clock, my sister came down to the library in a very charming wrap, and I soon found that she was as insensible to my presence as the others. I trembled with rage to see her kneel down by the coffin—my coffin, but when she bent over to kiss the pillow ,I threw away control.

A knife which had been used to cut string was lying upon a table: I seized it and drove it into her neck. She fled from the room screaming.

"Come! come!" she cried, her voice quivering with anguish. "The corpse is bleeding from the nose."

Then I cursed her.

On the evening of the third day, there was a heavy fall of snow. About eleven o'clock, I observed that the house was filled with blacks and mutes and folk of the county, who came for the obsequies. I went into the library and sat still, and waited. Soon came the men, and they closed the lid of the coffin and bore it out on their shoulders. And yet I sat, feeling rather sad that something of mine had been taken away: I could not quite think what. For half an hour perhaps—dreaming, dreaming: and then I glided to the hall door. There was no trace left of the funeral, but after a while, I sighted a black thread winding slowly across the white plain.

"I'm not dead!" I moaned, rubbed my face in the pure snow, and tossed it on my neck and hair. "Sweet God, I am not dead."

THE CASK OF AMONTILLADO

by Edgar Allan Poe

The thousand injuries of Fortunato I had borne as I best could, but when he ventured upon insult, I vowed revenge. You, who so well know the nature of my soul, will not suppose, however, that I gave utterance to a threat. At length, I would be avenged; this was a point definitely settled—but the very definitiveness with which it was resolved precluded the idea of risk. I must not only punish but punish with impunity. A wrong is unredressed when retribution overtakes its redresser. It is equally unredressed when the avenger fails to make himself feel as such to him who has done the wrong.

It must be understood that neither by word nor deed had I given Fortunato cause to doubt my goodwill. I continued, as was my wont, to smile in his face, and he did not perceive that my smile *now* was at the thought of his immolation.

He had a weak point—this Fortunato—although, in other regards, he was a man to be respected and even feared. He prided himself on his connoisseurship of wine. Few Italians have the true virtuoso spirit. For the most part, their enthusiasm is adopted to suit the time and opportunity—to practise imposture upon the British and Austrian *millionaires*. In painting and gemmary, Fortunato, like his countrymen, was a quack—but in the matter of old wines, he was sincere. In this respect, I did not differ from him materially: I was skillful in the Italian vintages and bought largely whenever I could.

It was about dusk, one evening during the supreme madness of the carnival season, that I encountered my friend. He accosted me with excessive warmth, for he had been drinking much. The man wore motley. He had on a tight-fitting party-striped dress, and his head was surmounted by the conical cap and bells. I was so pleased to see him that I thought I should never have done wringing his hand.

I said to him—"My dear Fortunato, you are luckily met. How remarkably well you are looking today! But I have received a pipe of what passes for Amontillado, and I have my doubts."

"How?" said he. "Amontillado? A pipe? Impossible! And in the middle of the carnival!"

"I have my doubts," I replied, "and I was silly enough to pay the full Amontillado price without consulting you in the matter. You were not to be found, and I was fearful of losing a bargain."

"Amontillado!"

"I have my doubts."

"Amontillado!"

"And I must satisfy them."

"Amontillado!"

"As you are engaged, I am on my way to Luchesi. If anyone has a critical turn, it is he. He will tell me—"

"Luchesi cannot tell Amontillado from Sherry."

"And yet some fools will have it that his taste is a match for your own."

"Come, let us go."

"Whither?"

"To your vaults."

"My friend, no, I will not impose upon your good nature. I perceive you have an engagement. Luchesi—"

"I have no engagement;—come."

"My friend, no. It is not the engagement but the severe cold with which I perceive you are afflicted. The vaults are insufferably damp. They are encrusted with nitre."

"Let us go, nevertheless. The cold is merely nothing. Amontillado! You have been imposed upon. And as for Luchesi, he cannot distinguish Sherry from Amontillado."

Thus speaking, Fortunato possessed himself of my arm. Putting on a mask of black silk and drawing a roquelaure closely about my person, I suffered him to hurry me to my palazzo.

There were no attendants at home; they had absconded to make merry in honour of the time. I had told them that I should not return until the morning and had given them explicit orders not to stir from the house. These orders were sufficient, I well knew, to ensure their immediate disappearance, one and all, as soon as my back was turned.

I took from their sconces two flambeaux, and, giving one to Fortunato, bowed him through several suites of rooms to the archway that led into the vaults. I passed down a long and winding staircase, requesting him to be cautious as he followed. We came at length to the foot of the descent and stood together on the damp ground of the catacombs of the Montresors.

The gait of my friend was unsteady, and the bells upon his cap jingled as he strode.

"The pipe," said he.

"It is farther on," said I, "but observe the white web-work which gleams from these cavern walls."

He turned towards me and looked into my eyes with two filmy orbs that distilled the rheum of intoxication.

"Nitre?" he asked at length.

"Nitre," I replied. "How long have you had that cough?"

"Ugh! ugh! ugh!—ugh! ugh! ugh!—ugh! ugh! ugh!—ugh! ugh! ugh!—ugh! ugh! ugh!"

My poor friend found it impossible to reply for many minutes.

"It is nothing," he said at last.

"Come," I said, with a decision, "we will go back; your health is precious. You are rich, respected, admired, beloved; you are happy, as once I was. You are a man to be missed. For me it is no matter. We will go back; you will be ill, and I cannot be responsible. Besides, there is Luchesi—"

"Enough," he said; "the cough is a mere nothing; it will not kill me. I shall not die of a cough."

"True—true," I replied, "and, indeed, I had no intention of alarming you unnecessarily—but you should use all proper caution. A draught of this Medoc will defend us from the damps."

Here I knocked off the neck of a bottle which I drew from a long row of its fellows that lay upon the mould.

"Drink," I said, presenting him with the wine.

He raised it to his lips with a leer. He paused and nodded to me familiarly while his bells jingled.

"I drink," he said, "to the buried that repose around us."

"And I to your long life."

He again took my arm, and we proceeded.

"These vaults," he said, "are extensive."

"The Montresors," I replied, "were a great and numerous family."

"I forget your arms."

"A huge human foot d'or, in a field azure; the foot crushes a serpent rampant whose fangs are imbedded in the heel."

"And the motto?"

"Nemo me impune lacessit."

"Good!" he said.

The wine sparkled in his eyes, and the bells jingled. My own fancy grew warm with the Medoc. We had passed through walls of piled bones, with casks and puncheons intermingling, into the inmost recesses of catacombs. I paused again, and this time I made bold to seize Fortunato by the arm above the elbow.

"The nitre!" I said, "see, it increases. It hangs like moss upon the vaults. We are below the river's bed. The drops of moisture trickle among the bones. Come, we will go back ere it is too late. Your cough—"

"It is nothing," he said; "let us go on. But first, another draught of the Medoc."

I broke and reached him a flagon of De Grave. He emptied it with a breath. His eyes flashed with a fierce light. He laughed and threw the bottle upwards with a gesticulation I did not understand.

I looked at him in surprise. He repeated the movement—a grotesque one.

"You do not comprehend?" he said.

"Not I," I replied.

"Then you are not of the brotherhood."

"How?"

"You are not of the masons."

"Yes, yes," I said; "yes, yes."

"You? Impossible! A mason?"

"A mason," I replied.

"A sign," he said, "a sign."

"It is this," I answered, producing a trowel from beneath the folds of my roquelaire.

"You jest," he exclaimed, recoiling a few paces. "But let us proceed to the Amontillado."

"Be it so," I said, replacing the tool beneath the cloak and again offering him my arm. He leaned upon it heavily. We continued our route in search of the Amontillado. We passed through a range of low arches, descended, passed on, and descending again, arrived at a deep crypt, in which the foulness of the air caused our flambeaux rather glow more than flame.

At the most remote end of the crypt, there appeared another less spacious. Its walls had been lined with human remains piled to the vault overhead in the fashion of the great catacombs of Paris. Three sides of this interior crypt were still ornamented in this manner. From the fourth side, the bones had been thrown down and lay promiscuously upon the earth, forming at one point a mound of some size. Within the wall thus exposed by the displacing of the bones, we perceived a still interior recess, in depth about four feet in width three, in height six or seven. It seemed to have been constructed for no especial use within itself but formed merely the interval between two of the colossal supports of the roof of the catacombs and was backed by one of their circumscribing walls of solid granite.

It was in vain that Fortunato, uplifting his dull torch, endeavoured to pry into the depth of the recess. Its termination, the feeble light, did not enable us to see.

"Proceed," I said; "herein is the Amontillado. As for Luchesi—"

"He is an ignoramus," interrupted my friend as he stepped unsteadily forward while I followed immediately at his heels. In an instant, he had reached the extremity of the niche and, finding his progress arrested by the rock, stood stupidly bewildered. A moment more, and I had fettered him to the granite. On its surface were two iron staples, distant from each other about two feet, horizontally. One of these depended on a short chain, from the other a padlock. Throwing the links about his waist, it was but the work of a few seconds to secure it. He was too astounded to resist. Withdrawing the key, I stepped back from recess.

"Pass your hand," I said, "over the wall; you cannot help feeling the nitre. Indeed, it is *very* damp. Once more let me *implore* you to return. No? Then I must positively leave you. But I must first render you all the little attentions in my power."

"The Amontillado!" ejaculated my friend, not yet recovered from his astonishment.

"True," I replied, "the Amontillado."

As I said these words, I busied myself among the pile of bones of which I had before spoken. Throwing them aside, I soon uncovered a quantity of building stone and mortar. With these materials and with the aid of my trowel, I began vigorously to wall up the entrance of the niche.

I had scarcely laid the first tier of the masonry when I discovered that the intoxication of Fortunato had in a great measure worn off. The earliest indication I had of this was a low moaning cry from the depth of the recess. It was not the cry of a drunken man. There was then a long and obstinate silence. I laid the second tier, the third, and the fourth, and then I heard the furious vibrations of the chain. The noise lasted for several minutes, during which, that I might hearken to it with the more satisfaction, I ceased my labours and sat down upon the bones. When at last the clanking subsided, I resumed the trowel and finished without interruption the fifth, the sixth, and the seventh tier. The wall was now nearly upon a level with my breast. I again paused and, holding the flambeaux over the mason work, threw a few feeble rays upon the figure within.

A succession of loud and shrill screams, bursting suddenly from the throat of the chained form, seemed to thrust me violently back. For a brief moment, I hesitated—I trembled. Unsheathing my rapier, I began to grope with it about the recess, but the thought of an instant reassured me. I placed my hand upon the solid fabric of the catacombs and felt satisfied. I reapproached the wall; I replied to the yells of him who clamoured. I re-echoed—I aided—I surpassed them in volume and in strength. I did this, and the clamourer grew still.

It was now midnight, and my task was drawing to a close. I had completed the eighth, the ninth, and the tenth tier. I had finished a portion of the last and the eleventh; there remained but a single stone to be fitted and plastered in. I struggled with its weight; I placed it partially in its destined position. But now there came from out the niche a low laugh that erected the hairs upon my head. It was succeeded by a sad voice, which I had difficulty recognizing as that of the noble Fortunato. The voice said—

"Ha! ha! ha!—he! he! he!—a very good joke indeed— an excellent jest. We shall have many a rich laugh about it at the palazzo—he! he! he!—over our wine—he! he! he!"

"The Amontillado!" I said.

"He! he! he!—he! he! he!—yes, the Amontillado. But is it not getting late? Will not they be awaiting us at the palazzo, the Lady Fortunato and the rest? Let us be gone."

"Yes," I said, "let us be gone."

"For the love of God, Montresor!"

"Yes," I said, "for the love of God!"

But to these words, I hearkened in vain for a reply. I grew impatient. I called aloud—

"Fortunato!"

No answer. I called again—

"Fortunato—"

No answer still. I thrust a torch through the remaining aperture and let it fall within. There came forth in reply only a jingling of the bells. My heart grew sick on account of the dampness of the catacombs. I hastened to make an end of my labour. I forced the last stone into its position; I plastered it up. Against the new masonry, I re-erected the old rampart of bones. For half of a century, no mortal has disturbed them. In pace requiescat!

THE VAMPYRE

by John William Polidori

It happened that in the midst of the dissipations attendant upon a London winter, there appeared at the various parties of the leaders of the ton a nobleman, more remarkable for his singularities than his rank. He gazed upon the mirth around him as if he could not participate therein. Apparently, the light laughter of the fair only attracted his attention, that he might, by a look, quell it and throw fear into those breasts where thoughtlessness reigned. Those who felt this sensation of awe could not explain whence it arose: some attributed it to the dead grey eye, which, fixing upon the object's face, did not seem to penetrate and, at one glance to pierce through to the inward workings of the heart; but fell upon the cheek with a leaden ray that weighed upon the skin it could not pass. His peculiarities caused him to be invited to every house; all wished to see him, and those who had been accustomed to violent excitement and now felt the weight of ennui, were pleased at having something in their presence capable of engaging their attention. In spite of the deadly hue of his face, which never gained a warmer tint, either from the blush of modesty, or from the strong emotion of passion, though its form and outline were beautiful, many of the female hunters, after notoriety, attempted to win his attentions, and gain, at least, some marks of what they might term affection: Lady Mercer, who had been the mockery of every monster shown in drawing-rooms since her marriage, threw herself in his way, and did all but put on the dress of a mountebank, to attract his notice:—though in vain:—when she stood before him, though his eyes were apparently fixed upon her's, still it seemed as if they were unperceived;—even her unappalled impudence was baffled, and she left the field. But though the common adultress could not influence even the guidance of his eyes, it was not that the female sex was indifferent to him: yet such was the apparent caution with which he spoke to the virtuous wife and innocent daughter that few knew he ever addressed himself to females. He had, however, the reputation of a winning tongue, and whether it was that it even overcame the dread of his singular character or that they were moved by his apparent hatred of vice, he was as often among those females who form the boast of their sex from their domestic virtues, as among those who sully it by their vices.

About the same time, there came to London a young gentleman by the name of Aubrey: he was an orphan left with an only sister in possession of great wealth by parents who died while he was yet in childhood. Left also to himself by guardians, who thought it their duty merely to take care of his fortune, while they relinquished the more important charge of his mind to the care of mercenary subalterns, he cultivated more his imagination than his judgment. He had, hence, that high romantic feeling of honour and candour, which daily ruins so many milliners' apprentices. He believed all to sympathise with virtue and thought that vice was thrown in by Providence merely for the picturesque effect of the scene, as we see in romances: he thought that the misery of a cottage merely consisted in the vesting of clothes, which were as warm, but which were better adapted to the painter's eye by their irregular folds and various colored patches. He thought, in fine, that the dreams of poets were the realities of life. He was handsome, frank, and rich: for these reasons, upon his entering into the gay circles, many mothers surrounded him, striving should describe with least truth their languishing or romping favourites: the daughters at the same time, by their brightening countenances when he approached, and by their sparkling eyes, when he opened his lips, soon led him into false notions of his talents and his merit. Attached as he was to the romance of his solitary hours, he was startled at finding, that, except in the tallow and wax candles that flickered, not from the presence of a ghost, but from want of snuffing, there was no foundation in real life for any of that congeries of pleasing pictures and descriptions contained in those volumes, from which he had formed his study. Finding, however, some compensation for his gratified vanity, he was about to relinquish his dreams when the extraordinary being we have above described, crossed him in his career.

He watched him; and the very impossibility of forming an idea of the character of a man entirely absorbed in himself, who gave few other signs of his observation of external objects, then the tacit assent to their existence implied by the avoidance of their contact: allowing his imagination to picture everything that flattered its propensity to extravagant ideas, he soon formed this object into the hero of a romance, and determined to observe the offspring of his fancy, rather than the person before him. He became acquainted with him, paid him attention, and so far advanced upon his notice that his presence was always recognized. He gradually learnt that Lord Ruthven's affairs were embarrassing and soon found, from the notes of preparation in —— Street, that he was about to travel. Desirous of gaining some information respecting this singular character, who, till now, had only whetted his curiosity, he hinted to his guardians that it was time for him to perform the tour, which for many generations has been thought necessary to enable the young to take some rapid steps in the career of vice towards putting themselves upon an equality with the aged, and not allowing them to appear as if fallen from the skies, whenever scandalous intrigues are mentioned as the subjects of pleasantry or praise, according to the degree of skill shown in carrying them on. They consented: and Aubrey, immediately mentioning his intentions to Lord Ruthven, was surprised to receive from him a proposal to join him. Flattered by such a mark of esteem from him, who, apparently, had nothing in common with other men, he gladly accepted it, and in a few days, they had passed the circling waters.

Hitherto, Aubrey had had no opportunity of studying Lord Ruthven's character, and now he found that, though many more of his actions were exposed to his view, the results offered different conclusions from the apparent motives to his conduct. His companion was profuse in his liberality;—the idle, the vagabond, and the beggar received from his hand more than enough to relieve their immediate wants. But Aubrey could not avoid remarking, that it was not upon the virtuous, reduced to indigence by the misfortunes attendant even upon virtue, that he bestowed his alms;—these were sent from the door with hardly suppressed sneers; but when the profligate came to ask something, not to relieve his wants, but to allow him to wallow in his lust, or to sink him still deeper in his iniquity, he was sent away with rich charity. This was, however, attributed by him to the greater importunity of the vicious, which generally prevails over the retiring bashfulness of the virtuous indigent. There was one circumstance about the charity of his Lordship, which was still more impressed upon his mind: all those upon whom it was bestowed inevitably found that there was a curse upon it, for they were all either led to the scaffold or sunk to the lowest and the most abject misery. At Brussels and other towns through which they passed, Aubrey was surprised at the apparent eagerness with which his companion sought for the centres of all fashionable vice; there he entered into all the spirit of the faro table: he betted, and always gambled with success, except where the known sharper was his antagonist, and then he lost even more than he gained; but it was always with the same unchanging face, with which he generally watched the society around: it was not, however, so when he encountered the rash youthful novice or the luckless father of a numerous family; then his very wish seemed fortune's law—this apparent abstractedness of mind was laid aside, and his eyes sparkled with more fire than that of the cat whilst dallying with the half-dead mouse. In every town, he left the formerly affluent youth, torn from the circle he adorned, cursing, in the solitude of a dungeon, the fate that had drawn him within the reach of this fiend; whilst many a father sat frantic, amidst the speaking looks of mute hungry children, without a single farthing of his late immense wealth, wherewith to buy even sufficient to satisfy their present craving. Yet he took no money from the gambling table; but immediately lost, to the ruiner of many, the last gilder he had just snatched from the convulsive grasp of the innocent: this might but be the result of a certain degree of knowledge, which was not, however, capable of combating the cunning of the more experienced. Aubrey often wished to represent this to his friend and beg him to resign that charity and pleasure which proved the ruin of all and did not tend to his own profit;—but he delayed it—for each day, he hoped his friend would give him some opportunity of speaking frankly and openly to him; however, this never occurred. Lord Ruthven in his carriage and amidst the various wild and rich scenes of nature, was always the same: his eye spoke less than his lip, and though Aubrey was near the object of his curiosity, he obtained no greater gratification from it than the constant excitement of vainly wishing to break that mystery, which to his exalted imagination began to assume the appearance of something supernatural.

They soon arrived at Rome, and Aubrey, for a time, lost sight of his companion; he left him in daily attendance upon the morning circle of an Italian countess whilst he went in search of the memorials of another almost deserted city. Whilst he was thus engaged, letters arrived from England, which he opened with eager impatience; the first was from his sister, breathing nothing but affection; the others were from his guardians, the latter astonished him; if it had before entered into his imagination that there was an evil power resident in his companion, these seemed to give him sufficient reason for the belief. His guardians insisted upon his immediately leaving his friend and urged that his character was dreadfully vicious, for the possession of irresistible powers of seduction rendered his licentious habits more dangerous to society. It had been discovered that his contempt for the adultress had not originated in hatred of her character; but that he had required, to enhance his gratification, that his victim, the partner of his guilt, should be hurled from the pinnacle of unsullied virtue, down to the lowest abyss of infamy and degradation: in fine, that all those females whom he had sought, apparently on account of their virtue, had, since his departure, thrown even the mask aside, and had not scrupled to expose the whole deformity of their vices to the public gaze.

Aubrey determined upon leaving one whose character had not yet shown a single bright point on which to rest the eye. He resolved to invent some plausible pretext for abandoning him altogether, purposing, in the meanwhile, to watch him more closely and to let no slight circumstances pass by unnoticed. He entered into the same circle and soon perceived that his Lordship was endeavouring to work upon the inexperience of the daughter of the lady whose house he chiefly frequented. In Italy, it is seldom that an unmarried female is met with in society; he was therefore obliged to carry on his plans in secret, but Aubrey's eye followed him in all his windings and soon discovered that an assignation had been appointed, which would most likely end in the ruin of an innocent, though thoughtless girl. Losing no time, he entered the apartment of Lord Ruthven and abruptly asked him his intentions with respect to the lady, informing him at the same time that he was aware of his being about to meet her that very night. Lord Ruthven answered that his intentions were such as he supposed all would have upon such an occasion, and upon being pressed whether he intended to marry her, merely laughed. Aubrey retired; and, immediately writing a note to say that from that moment, he must decline accompanying his Lordship in the remainder of their proposed tour, he ordered his servant to seek other apartments and, calling upon the mother of the lady, informed her of all he knew, not only with regard to her daughter but also concerning the character of his Lordship. The assignation was prevented. Lord Ruthven next day, merely sent his servant to notify his complete assent to a separation; but did not hint any suspicion of his plans having been foiled by Aubrey's interposition.

Having left Rome, Aubrey directed his steps towards Greece and, crossing the Peninsula, soon found himself at Athens. He then fixed his residence in the house of a Greek;

and soon occupied himself in tracing the faded records of ancient glory upon monuments that, apparently, ashamed of chronicling the deeds of freemen only before slaves had hidden beneath the sheltering soil or many colored lichen. Under the same roof as himself existed a being so beautiful and delicate that she might have formed the model for a painter wishing to portray on canvass the promised hope of the faithful in Mahomet's paradise, save that her eyes spoke too much mind for anyone to think she could belong to those who had no souls. As she danced upon the plain or tripped along the mountain's side, one would have thought the gazelle a poor type of her beauties; for who would have exchanged her eye, apparently the eye of animated nature, for that sleepy luxurious look of the animal suited but to the taste of an epicure. The light step of Ianthe often accompanied Aubrey in his search after antiquities, and often would the unconscious girl, engaged in the pursuit of a Kashmere butterfly, show the whole beauty of her form, floating as it were upon the wind, to the eager gaze of him, who forgot the letters he had just deciphered upon an almost effaced tablet, in the contemplation of her sylph-like figure. Often would her tresses falling, as she flitted around, exhibit in the sun's ray such delicately brilliant and swiftly fading hues, it might well excuse the forgetfulness of the antiquary, who let escape from his mind the very object he had before thought of vital importance to the proper interpretation of a passage in Pausanias. But why to attempt to describe charms which all feel but none can appreciate?—It was innocence, youth, and beauty, unaffected by crowded drawing rooms and stifling balls. Whilst he drew those remains of which he wished to preserve a memorial for his future hours, she would stand by and watch the magic effects of his pencil in tracing the scenes of her native place; she would then describe to him the circling dance upon the open plain, would paint, to him in all the glowing colors of youthful memory, the marriage pomp she remembered viewing in her infancy; and then, turning to subjects that had evidently made a greater impression upon her mind, would tell him all the supernatural tales of her nurse. Her earnestness and apparent belief of what she narrated excited the interest even of Aubrey, and often as she told him the tale of the living vampyre, who had passed years amidst his friends, and dearest ties, forced every year by feeding upon the life of a lovely female to prolong his existence for the ensuing months, his blood would run cold, whilst he attempted to laugh her out of such idle and horrible fantasies; but Ianthe cited to him the names of old men, who had, at last, detected one living among themselves after several of their near relatives and children had been found marked with the stamp of the fiend's appetite; and when she found him so incredulous, she begged of him to believe her, for it had been, remarked, that those who had dared to question their existence, always had some proof given, which obliged them, with grief and heartbreaking, to confess it was true. She detailed to him the traditional appearance of these monsters, and his horror was increased by hearing a pretty accurate description of Lord Ruthven; he, however, still persisted in persuading her that there could be no truth in her fears, though at the same time he wondered at the many coincidences which had all tended to excite a belief in the supernatural power of Lord Ruthven.

Aubrey began to attach himself more and more to Ianthe; her innocence, so contrasted with all the affected virtues of the women among whom he had sought for his vision of romance, won his heart; and while he ridiculed the idea of a young man of English habits, marrying an uneducated Greek girl, still he found himself more and more attached to the almost fairy form before him. He would tear himself at times from her, and, forming a plan for some antiquarian research, he would depart, determined not to return until his object was attained; but he always found it impossible to fix his attention upon the ruins around him, whilst in his mind, he retained an image that seemed alone the rightful possessor of his thoughts. Ianthe was unconscious of his love and was ever the same frank infantile being he had first known. She always seemed to part from him with reluctance, but it was because she no longer had anyone with whom she could visit her favourite haunts whilst her guardian was occupied in sketching or uncovering some fragment which had yet escaped the destructive hand of time. She had appealed to her parents on the subject of Vampyres, and they both, with several presents, affirmed their existence, pale with horror at the very name. Soon after, Aubrey determined to proceed upon one of his excursions, which was to detain him for a few hours; when they heard the name of the place, they all at once begged of him not to return at night, as he must necessarily pass through a wood, where no Greek would ever remain, after the day had closed, upon any consideration. They described it as the resort of the vampyres in their nocturnal orgies and denounced the most heavy evils as impending upon him who dared to cross their path. Aubrey made light of their representations and tried to laugh them out of the idea, but when he saw them shudder at his daring thus to mock a superior, infernal power, the very name of which apparently made their blood freeze, he was silent.

The next morning, Aubrey set off upon his excursion unattended; he was surprised to observe the melancholy face of his host and was concerned to find that his words, mocking the belief of those horrible fiends, had inspired them with such terror. When he was about to depart, Ianthe came to the side of his horse and earnestly begged of him to return, ere night allowed the power of these beings to be put in action;—he promised. He was, however, so occupied in his research, that he did not perceive that daylight would soon end and that on the horizon there was one of those specks which, in the warmer climates, so rapidly gather into a tremendous mass, and pour all their rage upon the devoted country.—He at last, however, mounted his horse, determined to make up by speed for his delay: but it was too late. Twilight, in these southern climates, is almost unknown; immediately the sun sets, the night begins: and ere he had advanced far, the power of the storm was above—its echoing thunders had scarcely an interval of rest—its thick heavy rain forced its way through the canopying foliage, whilst the blue forked lightning seemed to fall and radiate at his very feet. Suddenly his horse took fright, and he was carried with dreadful rapidity through the entangled forest. The animal at last, through fatigue, stopped, and he found, by the glare of lightning, that he was in the neighbourhood of a hovel that hardly lifted itself up from the masses of dead leaves and brushwood which surrounded it. Dismounting, he approached, hoping to find someone to guide him to the town or at least trust to obtain shelter from the pelting of the storm. As he approached, the thunders, for a moment silent, allowed him to hear the dreadful shrieks of a woman mingling with the stifled, exultant mockery of a laugh, continued in one almost unbroken sound;—he was startled: but, roused by the thunder which again rolled over his head, he, with a sudden effort, forced open the door of the hut. He found himself in utter darkness: the sound, however, guided him. He was apparently unperceived; for, though he called, still the sounds continued, and no notice was taken of him. He found himself in contact with someone, whom he immediately seized; when a voice cried, "Again baffled!" to which a loud laugh succeeded, and he felt grappled by one whose strength seemed superhuman: determined to sell his life as dearly as he could, he struggled, but it was in vain: he was lifted from his feet and hurled with enormous force against the ground:—his enemy threw himself upon him, and kneeling upon his breast, had placed his hands upon his throat—when the glare of many torches penetrating through the hole that gave light in the day, disturbed him;—he instantly rose, and, leaving his prey, rushed through the door, and in a moment the crashing of the branches, as he broke through the wood, was no longer heard. The storm was now still, and Aubrey, incapable of moving, was soon heard by those without. They entered; the light of their torches fell upon the mud walls, and the thatch loaded on every individual straw with heavy flakes of soot. At the desire of Aubrey, they searched for her who had attracted him by her cries; he was again left in darkness, but what was his horror, when the light of the torches once more burst upon him, to perceive the airy form of his fair conductress brought in a lifeless corpse. He shut his eyes, hoping that it was but a vision arising from his disturbed imagination, but he again saw the same form when he unclosed them, stretched by his side. There was no color upon her cheek, not even upon her lip, yet there was a stillness about her face that seemed almost as attaching as the life that once dwelt there:—upon her neck and breast was blood, and upon her throat were the marks of teeth having opened the vein:—to this the men pointed, crying, simultaneously struck with horror, "A Vampyre! a Vampyre!" A litter was quickly formed, and Aubrey was laid by the side of her who had lately been to him the object of so many bright and fairy visions, now fallen with the flower of life that had died within her. He knew not what his thoughts were—his mind was benumbed and seemed to shun reflection and take refuge in vacancy—he held almost unconsciously in his hand a naked dagger of a particular construction, which had been found in the hut. They were soon met by different parties who had been engaged in the search for her, whom a mother had missed. Their lamentable cries, as they approached the city, forewarned the parents of some dreadful catastrophe. —To describe their grief would be impossible, but when they ascertained the cause of their child's death, they looked at

Aubrey and pointed to the corpse. They were inconsolable; both died broken-hearted.

Aubrey being put to bed, was seized with a most violent fever and was often delirious; in these intervals, he would call upon Lord Ruthven and upon Ianthe—by some unaccountable combination, he seemed to beg of his former companion to spare the being he loved. At other times he would imprecate maledictions upon his head and curse him as her destroyer. Lord Ruthven chanced at this time to arrive at Athens and, from whatever motive, upon hearing of the state of Aubrey, immediately placed himself in the same house and became his constant attendant. When the latter recovered from his delirium, he was horrified and startled at the sight of him whose image he had now combined with that of a Vampyre; but Lord Ruthven, by his kind words, implied almost repentance for the fault that had caused their separation, and still more by the attention, anxiety, and care which he showed, soon reconciled him to his presence. His lordship seemed quite changed; he no longer appeared that apathetic being who had so astonished Aubrey, but as soon as his convalescence began to be rapid, he again gradually retired into the same state of mind, and Aubrey perceived no difference from the former man, except that at times he was surprised to meet his gaze fixed intently upon him, with a smile of malicious exultation playing upon his lips: he knew not why, but this smile haunted him. During the last stage of the invalid's recovery, Lord Ruthven was apparently engaged in watching the tideless waves raised by the cooling breeze or in marking the progress of those orbs, circling, like our world, the moveless sun;—indeed, he appeared to wish to avoid the eyes of all.

Aubrey's mind, by this shock, was much weakened, and that elasticity of spirit which had once so distinguished him now seemed to have fled forever. He was now as much a lover of solitude and silence as Lord Ruthven, but much as he wished for solitude, his mind could not find it in the neighbourhood of Athens; if he sought it amidst the ruins he had formerly frequented, Ianthe's form stood by his side —if he sought it in the woods, her light step would appear wandering amidst the underwood, in quest of the modest violet; then suddenly turning round, would show, to his wild imagination, her pale face and wounded throat, with a meek smile upon her lips. He determined to fly scenes, every feature of which created such bitter associations in his mind. He proposed to Lord Ruthven, to whom he held himself bound by the tender care he had taken of him during his illness, that they should visit those parts of Greece neither had yet seen. They travelled in every direction and sought every spot to which a recollection could be attached: but though they thus hastened from place to place, they seemed not to heed what they gazed upon. They heard much of robbers, but they gradually began to slight these reports, which they imagined were only the invention of individuals whose interest it was to excite the generosity of those whom they defended from pretended dangers. In consequence of thus neglecting the advice of the inhabitants, on one occasion, they travelled with only a few guards, more to serve as guides than as a defence. Upon entering, however, a narrow defile, at the bottom of which was the bed of a torrent, with large masses of rock brought down from the neighbouring precipices, they had reason to repent their negligence; for scarcely was the whole of the party engaged in the narrow pass, when they were startled by the whistling of bullets close to their heads, and by the echoed report of several guns. In an instant, their guards had left them and, placing themselves behind rocks, had begun to fire in the direction whence the report came. Lord Ruthven and Aubrey, imitating their example, retired for a moment behind the sheltering turn of the defile: but ashamed of being thus detained by a foe, who with insulting shouts bade them advance, and being exposed to unresisting slaughter, if any of the robbers should climb above and take them in the rear, they determined at once to rush forward in search of the enemy. Hardly had they lost the shelter of the rock when Lord Ruthven received a shot in the shoulder, which brought him to the ground. Aubrey hastened to his assistance; and, no longer heeding the contest or his own peril, was soon surprised by seeing the robbers' faces around him—his guards having, upon Lord Ruthven's being wounded, immediately thrown up their arms and surrendered.

By promises of great reward, Aubrey soon induced them to convey his wounded friend to a neighbouring cabin; and having agreed upon a ransom, he was no more disturbed by their presence—they being content merely to guard the entrance till their comrade should return with the promised sum, for which he had an order. Lord Ruthven's strength rapidly decreased; in two days, mortification ensued, and death seemed to advance with hasty steps. His conduct and appearance had not changed; he seemed as unconscious of pain as he had been of the objects about him: but towards the close of the last evening, his mind became apparently uneasy, and his eye often fixed upon Aubrey, who was induced to offer his assistance with more than usual earnestness—"Assist me! you may save me—you may do more than that—I mean not my life, I heed the death of my existence as little as that of the passing day; but you may save my honour, your friend's honour."—"How? tell me how? I would do any thing," replied Aubrey.—"I need but little—my life ebbs apace—I cannot explain the whole—but if you would conceal all you know of me, my honour were free from stain in the world's mouth—and if my death were unknown for some time in England—I—I—but life."—"It shall not be known."—"Swear!" cried the dying man, raising himself with exultant violence, "Swear by all your soul reveres, by all your nature fears, swear that, for a year and a day you will not impart your knowledge of my crimes or death to any living being in any way, whatever may happen, or whatever you may see. "—His eyes seemed bursting from their sockets: "I swear!" said Aubrey; he sunk laughing upon his pillow, and breathed no more.

Aubrey retired to rest, but did not sleep; the many circumstances attending his acquaintance with this man rose upon his mind, and he knew not why; when he remembered his oath a cold shivering came over him, as if from the presentiment of something horrible awaiting him. Rising early in the morning, he was about to enter the hovel in which he had left the corpse, when a robber met him and informed him that it was no longer there, having been conveyed by himself and comrades, upon his retiring, to the pinnacle of a neighbouring mount, according to a promise they had given his lordship, that it should be exposed to the first cold ray of the moon that rose after his death. Aubrey was astonished and, taking several of the men, determined to go and bury it upon the spot where it lay. But, when he had mounted to the summit, he found no trace of either the corpse or the clothes, though the robbers swore they pointed out the identical rock on which they had laid the body. For a time, his mind was bewildered in conjectures, but he at last returned, convinced that they had buried the corpse for the sake of the clothes.

Weary of a country in which he had met with such terrible misfortunes and in which all apparently conspired to heighten that superstitious melancholy that had seized upon his mind, he resolved to leave it and soon arrived at Smyrna. While waiting for a vessel to convey him to Otranto or to Naples, he occupied himself in arranging those effects he had with him belonging to Lord Ruthven. Amongst other things, there was a case containing several weapons of offence, more or less adapted to ensure the death of the victim. There were several daggers and ataghans. Whilst turning them over, and examining their curious forms, what was his surprise at finding a sheath apparently ornamented in the same style as the dagger discovered in the fatal hut—he shuddered—hastening to gain further proof, he found the weapon, and his horror may be imagined when he discovered that it fitted, though peculiarly shaped, the sheath he held in his hand. His eyes seemed to need no further certainty—they seemed to gaze to be bound to the dagger, yet still, he wished to disbelieve; but the particular form, the same varying tints upon the haft and sheath were alike in splendour on both, and left no room for doubt; there were also drops of blood on each.

He left Smyrna, and on his way home to Rome, his first inquiries were concerning the lady he had attempted to snatch from Lord Ruthven's seductive arts. Her parents were in distress, their fortune ruined, and she had not been heard of since the departure of his lordship. Aubrey's mind became almost broken under so many repeated horrors; he was afraid that this lady had fallen victim to the destroyer of Ianthe. He became morose and silent, and his only occupation consisted in urging the speed of the postilions as if he were going to save the life of someone he held dear. He arrived at Calais; a breeze, which seemed obedient to his will, soon wafted him to the English shores; and he hastened to the mansion of his fathers, and there, for a moment, appeared to lose, in the embraces and caresses of his sister, all memory of the past. If she before, by her infantine caresses, had gained his affection, now that the woman began to appear, she was still more attaching as a companion.

Miss Aubrey had not that winning grace which gains the gaze and applause of the drawing-room assemblies. There was none of that light brilliancy which only exists in the heated atmosphere of a crowded apartment. Her blue eye was never lit up by the levity of the mind beneath. There was a melancholy charm about it which did not seem to arise from misfortune but from some feeling within that appeared to indicate a soul conscious of a brighter realm.

Her step was not that light footing, which strays where'er a butterfly or a color might attract—it was sedate and pensive. When alone, her face was never brightened by the smile of joy; but when her brother breathed to her his affection and would in her presence forget those griefs she knew destroyed his rest, who would have exchanged her smile for that of the voluptuary? It seemed as if those eyes —that face were then playing in the light of their own native sphere. She was yet only eighteen and had not been presented to the world, it having been thought by her guardians more fit that her presentation should be delayed until her brother's return from the continent when he might be her protector. It was now, therefore, resolved that the next drawing room, which was fast approaching, should be the epoch of her entry into the "busy scene." Aubrey would rather have remained in the mansion of his fathers and fed upon the melancholy which overpowered him. He could not feel interested in the frivolities of fashionable strangers when his mind had been so torn by the events he had witnessed, but he determined to sacrifice his own comfort for the protection of his sister. They soon arrived in town and prepared for the next day, which had been announced as a drawing room.

The crowd was excessive—a drawing room had not been held for a long time, and all who were anxious to bask in the smile of royalty hastened thither. Aubrey was there with his sister. While he was standing in a corner by himself, heedless of all around him, engaged in the remembrance that the first time he had seen Lord Ruthven was in that very place—he felt suddenly seized by the arm, and a voice he recognized too well, sounded in his ear —"Remember your oath." He had hardly the courage to turn, fearful of seeing a spectre that would blast him when he perceived, at a little distance, the same figure which had attracted his notice on this spot upon his first entry into society. He gazed till his limbs almost refused to bear their weight. He was obliged to take the arm of a friend, and forcing a passage through the crowd, he threw himself into his carriage and was driven home. He paced the room with hurried steps and fixed his hands upon his head as if he were afraid his thoughts were bursting from his brain. Lord Ruthven again before him—circumstances started up in dreadful array—the dagger—his oath.—He roused himself, he could not believe it possible—the dead rise again!—He thought his imagination had conjured up the image his mind was resting upon. It was impossible that it could be real—he determined, therefore, to go again into society; for though he attempted to ask concerning Lord Ruthven, the name hung upon his lips, and he could not succeed in gaining information. He went a few nights after with his sister to the assembly of a near relation. Leaving her under the protection of a matron, he retired into a recess and there gave himself up to his own devouring thoughts. Perceiving, at last, that many were leaving, he roused himself and, entering another room, found his sister surrounded by several, apparently in earnest conversation; he attempted to pass and get near her when one, whom he requested to move, turned round and revealed to him those features he most abhorred. He sprang forward, seized his sister's arm, and, with a hurried step, forced her towards the street: at the door, he found himself impeded by the crowd of servants who were waiting for their lords, and while he was engaged in passing them, he again heard that voice whisper close to him—"Remember your oath!"—He did not dare to turn, but, hurrying his sister, soon reached home.

Aubrey became almost distracted. If before his mind had been absorbed by one subject, how much more completely was it engrossed now that the certainty of the monster's living again pressed upon his thoughts? His sister's attentions were now unheeded, and it was in vain that she intreated him to explain to her what had caused his abrupt conduct. He only uttered a few words, and those terrified her. The more he thought, the more he was bewildered. His oath startled him;—was he then to allow this monster to roam, bearing ruin upon his breath, amidst all he held dear, and not avert its progress? His very sister might have been touched by him. But even if he were to break his oath and disclose his suspicions, who would believe him? He thought of employing his own hand to free the world from such a wretch, but death, he remembered, had been already mocked. For days he remained in this state; shut up in his room, he saw no one and ate only when his sister came, who, with eyes streaming with tears, besought him, for her sake, to support nature. At last, no longer capable of bearing stillness and solitude, he left his house and roamed from street to street, anxious to fly that image which haunted him. His dress became neglected, and he wandered, as often exposed to the noon-day sun as to the midnight damps. He was no longer to be recognized at first he returned with the evening to the house, but at last, he laid him down to rest wherever fatigue overtook him. His sister, anxious for his safety, employed people to follow him; but they were soon distanced by him, who fled from a pursuer swifter than any—from thought. His conduct, however, suddenly changed. Struck with the idea that he left by his absence the whole of his friends, with a fiend amongst them, of whose presence they were unconscious, he determined to enter again into society and watch him closely, anxious to forewarn, in spite of his oath, all whom Lord Ruthven approached with intimacy. But when he entered into a room, his haggard and suspicious looks were so striking, his inward shudderings so visible, that his sister was at last obliged to beg of him to abstain from seeking, for her sake, a society which affected him so strongly. When, however, remonstrance proved unavailing, the guardians thought proper to interpose, and, fearing that his mind was becoming alienated, they thought it high time to resume again that trust which had been before imposed upon them by Aubrey's parents.

Desirous of saving him from the injuries and sufferings he had daily encountered in his wanderings and of preventing him from exposing to the general eye those marks of what they considered folly, they engaged a physician to reside in the house and take constant care of him. He hardly appeared to notice it, so completely was his mind absorbed by one terrible subject. His incoherence became at last so great that he was confined to his chamber. There he would often lie for days, incapable of being roused. He had become emaciated. His eyes had attained a glassy lustre;—the only sign of affection and recollection remaining displayed itself upon the entry of his sister; then he would sometimes start, and, seizing her hands, with looks that severely afflicted her, he would desire her not to touch him. "Oh, do not touch him—if your love for me is aught, do not go near him!" When, however, she inquired to whom he referred, his only answer was, "True! true!" and again, he sank into a state whence not even she could rouse him. This lasted many months: gradually, however, as the year passed, his incoherences became less frequent, and his mind threw off a portion of its gloom, whilst his guardians observed that several times in the day, he would count upon his fingers a definite number, and then smile.

The time had nearly elapsed, when, upon the last day of the year, one of his guardians entering his room, began to converse with his physician upon the melancholy circumstance of Aubrey's being in so awful a situation, when his sister was going next day to be married. Instantly Aubrey's attention was attracted; he asked anxiously to whom. Glad of this mark of returning intellect, of which they feared he had been deprived, they mentioned the name of the Earl of Marsden. Thinking this was a young Earl whom he had met with in society, Aubrey seemed pleased and astonished them still more by his expressing his intention to be present at the nuptials and desiring to see his sister. They answered not, but in a few minutes, his sister was with him. He was apparently again capable of being affected by the influence of her lovely smile; for he pressed her to his breast and kissed her cheek, wet with tears, flowing at the thought of her brother's being once more alive to the feelings of affection. He began to speak with all his wonted warmth, and to congratulate her upon her marriage with a person so distinguished for rank and every accomplishment; when he suddenly perceived a locket upon her breast; opening it, what was his surprise at beholding the features of the monster who had so long influenced his life. He seized the portrait in a paroxysm of rage and trampled it underfoot. Upon her asking him why he thus destroyed the resemblance of her future husband, he looked as if he did not understand her—then seizing her hands and gazing at her with a frantic expression of countenance, he bade her swear that she would never wed this monster, for he—— But he could not advance—it seemed as if that voice again bade him remember his oath —he turned suddenly round, thinking Lord Ruthven was near him but saw no one. In the meantime, the guardians and physician, who had heard the whole and thought this was but a return of his disorder, entered and, forcing him from Miss Aubrey, desired her to leave him. He fell upon his knees to them. He implored he begged of them to delay but for one day. They, attributing this to the insanity they imagined had taken possession of his mind, endeavoured to pacify him, and retired.

Lord Ruthven had called the morning after the drawing room and had been refused by everyone else. When he heard of Aubrey's ill health, he readily understood himself to be the cause of it; but when he learned that he was deemed insane, his exultation and pleasure could hardly be concealed from those among whom he had gained this information. He hastened to the house of his former companion, and, by constant attendance and the pretence of great affection for the brother and interest in his fate, he gradually won the ear of Miss Aubrey. Who could resist his power? His tongue had dangers and toils to recount—could speak of himself as an individual having no sympathy with any being on the crowded earth, save with her to whom he addressed himself;—could tell how, since he knew her, his existence, had begun to seem worthy of preservation, if it were merely that he might listen to her soothing accents;—in fine, he knew so well how to use the serpent's art, or such was the will of fate, that he gained her affections. The title of the elder branch falling at length to him, he obtained an important embassy, which served as an excuse for hastening the marriage (in spite of her brother's deranged state,) which was to take place the very day before his departure for the continent.

Aubrey, when he was left by the physician and his guardians, attempted to bribe the servants, but in vain. He asked for pen and paper; it was given to him; he wrote a letter to his sister, conjuring her, as she valued her own happiness, her own honour, and the honour of those now in the grave who once held her in their arms as their hope and the hope of their house, to delay but for a few hours that marriage, on which he denounced the most heavy curses. The servants promised they would deliver it, but giving it to the physician, he thought it better not to harass the mind of Miss Aubrey anymore by what he considered the ravings of a maniac. The night passed on without rest to the busy inmates of the house, and Aubrey heard, with a horror that may more easily be conceived than described, the notes of busy preparation. Morning came, and the sound of carriages broke upon his ear. Aubrey grew almost frantic. The curiosity of the servants, at last, overcame their vigilance, and they gradually stole away, leaving him in the custody of a helpless old woman. He seized the opportunity, with one bound, was out of the room and, in a moment, found himself in the apartment where all were nearly assembled. Lord Ruthven was the first to perceive him: he immediately approached and, taking his arm by force, hurried him from the room, speechless with rage. When on the staircase, Lord Ruthven whispered in his ear —"Remember your oath, and know, if not my bride to day, your sister is dishonoured. Women are frail!" So saying, he pushed him towards his attendants, who, roused by the old woman, had come in search of him. Aubrey could no longer support himself; his rage, not finding a vent, had broken a blood vessel, and he was conveyed to bed. This was not mentioned to his sister, who was not present when he entered, as the physician was afraid of agitating her. The marriage was solemnized, and the bride and bridegroom left London.

Aubrey's weakness increased; the effusion of blood produced symptoms of the near approach of death. He desired his sister's guardians might be called, and when the midnight hour had struck, he related composedly what the reader has perused—he died immediately after.

The guardians hastened to protect Miss Aubrey, but when they arrived, it was too late. Lord Ruthven had disappeared, and Aubrey's sister had glutted the thirst of a VAMPYRE!

THE BODY SNATCHER

by Robert Louis Stevenson

Every night in the year, four of us sat in the small parlour of the George at Debenham—the undertaker, the landlord, Fettes, and myself. Sometimes there would be more, but blow high, blow low, come rain or snow or frost, we four would be each planted in his own particular armchair. Fettes was an old drunken Scotchman, a man of education obviously, and a man of some property since he lived in idleness. He had come to Debenham years ago, while still young, and by a mere continuance of living, had grown to be an adopted townsman. His blue camlet cloak was a local antiquity, like the church spire. His place in the parlour at the George, his absence from church, and his old, crapulous, disreputable vices were all things, of course, in Debenham. He had some vague

Radical opinions and some fleeting infidelities, which he would now and again set forth and emphasise with tottering slaps upon the table. He drank rum—five glasses regularly every evening; and, for the greater portion of his nightly visit to the George, sat with his glass in his right hand, in a state of melancholy alcoholic saturation. We called him the Doctor, for he was supposed to have some special knowledge of medicine, and had been known, upon a pinch, to set a fracture or reduce a dislocation, but beyond these slight particulars, we had no knowledge of his character and antecedents.

One dark winter night—it had struck nine sometime before the landlord joined us—there was a sick man in the George, a great neighbouring proprietor suddenly struck down with apoplexy on his way to Parliament, and the great man's still greater London doctor had been telegraphed to his bedside. It was the first time that such a thing had happened in Debenham, for the railway was but newly open, and we were all proportionately moved by the occurrence.

'He's come,' said the landlord after he had filled and lighted his pipe.

'He?' said I. 'Who?—not the doctor?'

'Himself,' replied our host.

'What is his name?'

'Doctor Macfarlane,' said the landlord.

Fettes was far through his third tumbler, stupidly fuddled, now nodding over, now staring mazily around him; but at the last word, he seemed to awaken and repeated the name 'Macfarlane' twice, quietly enough the first time, but with sudden emotion at the second.

'Yes,' said the landlord, 'that's his name, Doctor Wolfe Macfarlane.'

Fettes became instantly sober; his eyes awoke, his voice became clear, loud, and steady, and his language forcible and earnest. We were all startled by the transformation, as if a man had risen from the dead.

'I beg your pardon,' he said, 'I am afraid I have not been paying much attention to your talk. Who is this Wolfe Macfarlane?' And then, when he had heard the landlord out, 'It cannot be, it cannot be,' he added, 'and yet I would like well to see him face to face.'

'Do you know him, Doctor?' asked the undertaker with a gasp.

'God forbid!' was the reply. 'And yet the name is a strange one; it were too much to fancy two. Tell me, landlord, is he old?'

'Well,' said the host, 'he's not a young man, to be sure, and his hair is white; but he looks younger than you.'

'He is older, though; years older. But,' with a slap upon the table, 'it's the rum you see in my face—rum and sin. This man, perhaps, may have an easy conscience and a good digestion. Conscience! Hear me speak. You would think I was some good, old, decent Christian, would you not? But no, not I; I never canted. Voltaire might have canted if he'd stood in my shoes; but the brains'—with a rattling fillip on his bald head—'the brains were clear and active, and I saw and made no deductions.'

'If you know this doctor,' I ventured to remark, after a somewhat awful pause, 'I should gather that you do not share the landlord's good opinion.'

Fettes paid no regard to me.

'Yes,' he said, with sudden decision, 'I must see him face to face.'

There was another pause, and then a door was closed rather sharply on the first floor, and a step was heard upon the stair.

'That's the doctor,' cried the landlord. 'Look sharp, and you can catch him.'

It was but two steps from the small parlour to the door of the old George Inn; the wide oak staircase landed almost in the street; there was room for a Turkey rug and nothing more between the threshold and the last round of the descent; but this little space was every evening brilliantly lit up, not only by the light upon the stair and the great signal-lamp below the sign but by the warm radiance of the bar-room window. The George thus brightly advertised itself to passers-by in the cold street. Fettes walked steadily to the spot, and we, who were hanging behind, beheld the two men meet, as one of them had phrased it, face to face. Dr Macfarlane was alert and vigorous. His white hair set off his pale and placid, although energetic, countenance. He was richly dressed in the finest of broadcloth and the whitest of linen, with a great gold watch chain and studs and spectacles of the same precious material. He wore a broad-folded tie, white and speckled with lilac, and he carried on his arm a comfortable driving coat of fur. There was no doubt, but he became his years, breathing, as he did, of wealth and consideration, and it was a surprising contrast to see our parlour sot—bald, dirty, pimpled, and robed in his old camlet cloak—confront him at the bottom of the stairs.

'Macfarlane!' he said somewhat loudly, more like a herald than a friend.

The great doctor pulled up short on the fourth step as though the familiarity of the address surprised and somewhat shocked his dignity.

'Toddy Macfarlane!' repeated Fettes.

The London man almost staggered. He stared for the swiftest of seconds at the man before him, glanced behind him with a sort of scare, and then in a startled whisper, 'Fettes!' he said, 'You!'

'Ay,' said the other, 'me! Did you think I was dead too? We are not so easy shut of our acquaintance.'

'Hush, hush!' exclaimed the doctor. 'Hush, hush! this meeting is so unexpected—I can see you are unmanned. I hardly knew you, I confess, at first; but I am overjoyed—overjoyed to have this opportunity. For the present it must be how-d'ye-do and good-bye in one, for my fly is waiting, and I must not fail the train; but you shall—let me see—yes —you shall give me your address, and you can count on early news of me. We must do something for you, Fettes. I fear you are out at elbows; but we must see to that for auld lang syne, as once we sang at suppers.'

'Money!' cried Fettes; 'money from you! The money that I had from you is lying where I cast it in the rain.'

Dr Macfarlane had talked himself into some measure of superiority and confidence, but the uncommon energy of this refusal cast him back into his first confusion.

A horrible, ugly look came and went across his almost venerable countenance. 'My dear fellow,' he said, 'be it as you please; my last thought is to offend you. I would intrude on none. I will leave you my address, however—'

'I do not wish it—I do not wish to know the roof that shelters you,' interrupted the other. 'I heard your name; I feared it might be you; I wished to know if, after all, there were a God; I know now that there is none. Begone!'

He still stood in the middle of the rug, between the stair and doorway, and the great London physician, in order to escape, would be forced to step to one side. It was plain that he hesitated before the thought of this humiliation. White as he was, there was a dangerous glitter in his spectacles; but while he still paused uncertain, he became aware that the driver of his fly was peering in from the street at this unusual scene and caught a glimpse at the same time of our little body from the parlour, huddled by the corner of the bar. The presence of so many witnesses decided him at once to flee. He crouched together, brushing on the wainscot, and made a dart like a serpent, striking for the door. But his tribulation was not yet entirely at an end, for even as he was passing, Fettes clutched him by the arm, and these words came in a whisper, and yet painfully distinct, 'Have you seen it again?'

The great rich London doctor cried out aloud with a sharp, throttling cry; he dashed his questioner across the open space and, with his hands over his head, fled out of the door like a detected thief. Before it had occurred to one of us to make a movement the fly was already rattling toward the station. The scene was over like a dream, but the dream had left proof and traces of its passage. The next day the servant found the fine gold spectacles broken on the threshold, and that very night we were all standing breathless by the bar-room window, and Fettes at our side, sober, pale, and resolute in look.

'God protect us, Mr Fettes!' said the landlord, coming first into possession of his customary senses. 'What in the universe is all this? These are strange things you have been saying.'

Fettes turned toward us; he looked us each in succession in the face. 'See if you can hold your tongues,' said he. 'That man Macfarlane is not safe to cross; those that have done so already have repented it too late.'

And then, without so much as finishing his third glass, far less waiting for the other two, he bade us goodbye and went forth, under the lamp of the hotel, into the black night.

We three turned to our places in the parlour, with the big red fire and four clear candles, and as we recapitulated what had passed, the first chill of our surprise soon changed into a glow of curiosity. We sat late; it was the latest session I have known in the old George. Each man, before we parted, had his theory that he was bound to prove; and none of us had any nearer business in this world than to track out the past of our condemned companion and surprise the secret that he shared with the great London doctor. It is no great boast, but I believe I was a better hand at worming out a story than either of my fellows at the George, and perhaps there is now no other man alive who could narrate to you the following foul and unnatural events.

In his young days, Fettes studied medicine in the schools of Edinburgh. He had a talent of a kind, the talent that picks up swiftly what it hears and readily retails it for its own. He worked little at home, but he was civil, attentive, and intelligent in the presence of his masters. They soon picked him out as a lad who listened closely and remembered well; nay, strange as it seemed to me when I first heard it, he was in those days well favoured, and pleased by his exterior. There was, at that period, a certain extramural teacher of anatomy, whom I shall here designate by the letter K. His name was subsequently too well known. The man who bore it skulked through the streets of Edinburgh in disguise, while the mob that applauded at the execution of Burke called loudly for the blood of his employer. But Mr K— was then at the top of his vogue; he enjoyed popularity due partly to his own talent and address, partly to the incapacity of his rival, the university professor. The students, at least, swore by his name, and Fettes believed himself and was believed by others to have laid the foundations of success when he had acquired the favour of this meteorically famous man. Mr K— was a bon vivant as well as an accomplished teacher; he liked a sly illusion no less than a careful preparation. In both capacities, Fettes enjoyed and deserved his notice, and by the second year of his attendance, he held the half-regular position of second demonstrator or sub-assistant in his class.

In this capacity, the charge of the theatre and lecture room devolved in particular upon his shoulders. He had to answer for the cleanliness of the premises and the conduct of the other students, and it was a part of his duty to supply, receive, and divide the various subjects. It was with a view to this last—at that time very delicate— an affair that he was lodged by Mr K— in the same wynd and at last in the same building, with the dissecting rooms. Here, after a night of turbulent pleasures, his hand still tottering, his sight still misty and confused, he would be called out of bed in the black hours before the winter dawn by the unclean and desperate interlopers who supplied the table. He would open the door to these men since they were infamous throughout the land. He would help them with their tragic burden, pay them their sordid price, and remain alone when they were gone with the unfriendly relics of humanity. From such a scene, he would return to snatch another hour or two of slumber, to repair the abuses of the night, and refresh himself for the labours of the day.

Few lads could have been more insensible to the impressions of a life thus passed among the ensigns of mortality. His mind was closed against all general considerations. He was incapable of interest in the fate and fortunes of another, the slave of his own desires and low ambitions. Cold, light, and selfish in the last resort, he had that modicum of prudence, miscalled morality, which keeps a man from inconvenient drunkenness or punishable theft. He coveted, besides, a measure of consideration from his masters and his fellow pupils, and he had no desire to fail conspicuously in the external parts of life. Thus he made it his pleasure to gain some distinction in his studies and, day after day, rendered unimpeachable eye service to his employer, Mr K——. For his day of work, he indemnified himself by nights of roaring, blackguardly enjoyment, and when that balance had been struck, the organ that he called his conscience declared itself content.

The supply of subjects was a continual trouble to him as well as to his master. In that large and busy class, the raw material of the anatomists kept perpetually running out; and the business thus rendered necessary was not only unpleasant in itself but threatened dangerous consequences to all who were concerned. It was the policy of Mr K—— to ask no questions in his dealings with the trade. 'They bring the body, and we pay the price,' he used to say, dwelling on the alliteration—'quid pro quo.' And, again, and somewhat profanely, 'Ask no questions,' he would tell his assistants, 'for conscience' sake.' There was no understanding that the subjects were provided by the crime of murder. Had that idea been broached to him in words, he would have recoiled in horror; but the lightness of his speech upon so grave a matter was, in itself, an offence against good manners and a temptation to the men with whom he dealt. Fettes, for instance, had often remarked to himself upon the singular freshness of the bodies. He had been struck again and again by the hang dog abominable looks of the ruffians who came to him before the dawn, and putting things together clearly in his private thoughts; he perhaps attributed a meaning too immoral and too categorical to the unguarded counsels of his master. He understood his duty, in short, to have three branches: to take what was brought, to pay the price, and to avert the eye from any evidence of a crime.

One November morning this policy of silence was put sharply to the test. He had been awake all night with a racking toothache—pacing his room like a caged beast or throwing himself in fury on his bed—and had fallen at last into that profound, uneasy slumber that so often follows on a night of pain when he was awakened by the third or fourth angry repetition of the concerted signal. There was a thin, bright moonshine; it was bitter cold, windy, and frosty; the town had not yet awakened, but an indefinable stir already preluded the noise and business of the day. The ghouls had come later than usual, and they seemed more than usually eager to be gone. Fettes, sick with sleep, lighted them upstairs. He heard their grumbling Irish voices through a dream, and as they stripped the sack from their sad merchandise, he leaned dozing with his shoulder propped against the wall; he had to shake himself to find the men their money. As he did so, his eyes lighted on the dead face. He started; he took two steps nearer with the candle raised.

'God Almighty!' he cried. 'That is Jane Galbraith!'

The men answered nothing, but they shuffled nearer the door.

'I know her, I tell you,' he continued. 'She was alive and hearty yesterday. It's impossible she can be dead; it's impossible you should have got this body fairly.'

'Sure, sir, you're mistaken entirely,' said one of the men.

But the other looked Fettes darkly in the eyes and demanded the money on the spot.

It was impossible to misconceive the threat or to exaggerate the danger. The lad's heart failed him. He stammered some excuses, counted out the sum, and saw his hateful visitors depart. No sooner were they gone than he hastened to confirm his doubts. By a dozen unquestionable marks, he identified the girl he had jested with the day before. He saw, with horror, marks upon her body that might well betoken violence. A panic seized him, and he took refuge in his room. There he reflected at length over the discovery that he had made, considered soberly the bearing of Mr K—'s instructions and the danger to himself of interference in so serious a business, and at last, in sore perplexity, determined to wait for the advice of his immediate superior, the class assistant.

This was a young doctor, Wolfe Macfarlane, a high favourite among all the reckless students, clever, dissipated, and unscrupulous to the last degree. He had travelled and studied abroad. His manners were agreeable and a little forward. He was an authority on the stage, skilful on the ice or the links with a skate or golf club. He dressed with nice audacity, and, to put the finishing touch upon his glory, he kept a gig and a strong trotting horse. With Fettes he was on terms of intimacy. Indeed, their relative positions called for some community of life; and when subjects were scarce, the pair would drive far into the country in Macfarlane's gig, visit and desecrate some lonely graveyard, and return before dawn with their booty to the door of the dissecting room.

On that particular morning, Macfarlane arrived somewhat earlier than his wont. Fettes heard him, and met him on the stairs, told him his story, and showed him the cause of his alarm. Macfarlane examined the marks on her body.

'Yes,' he said with a nod, 'it looks fishy.'

'Well, what should I do?' asked Fettes.

'Do?' repeated the other. 'Do you want to do anything? Least said soonest mended, I should say.'

'Some one else might recognize her,' objected Fettes. 'She was as well known as the Castle Rock.'

'We'll hope not,' said Macfarlane, 'and if anybody does—well, you didn't, don't you see, and there's an end. The fact is, this has been going on too long. Stir up the mud, and you'll get K— into the most unholy trouble; you'll be in a shocking box yourself. So will I, if you come to that. I should like to know how any one of us would look, or what the devil we should have to say for ourselves, in any Christian witness-box. For me, you know there's one thing certain—that, practically speaking, all our subjects have been murdered.'

'Macfarlane!' cried Fettes.

'Come now!' sneered the other. 'As if you hadn't suspected it yourself!'

'Suspecting is one thing—'

'And proof another. Yes, I know; and I'm as sorry as you are this should have come here,' tapping the body with his cane. 'The next best thing for me is not to recognize it; and,' he added coolly, 'I don't. You may, if you please. I don't dictate, but I think a man of the world would do as I do; and I may add, I fancy that is what K— would look for at our hands. The question is, Why did he choose us two for his assistants? And I answer, because he didn't want old wives.'

This was the tone of all others to affect the mind of a lad like Fettes. He agreed to imitate Macfarlane. The body of the unfortunate girl was duly dissected, and no one remarked or appeared to recognize her.

One afternoon, when his day's work was over, Fettes dropped into a popular tavern and found Macfarlane sitting with a stranger. This was a small man, very pale and dark, with coal-black eyes. The cut of his features gave a promise of intellect and refinement, which was but feebly realized in his manners, for he proved, upon a nearer acquaintance, coarse, vulgar, and stupid. He exercised, however, very remarkable control over Macfarlane; issued orders like the Great Bashaw; became inflamed at the least discussion or delay, and commented rudely on the servility with which he was obeyed. This most offensive person took a fancy to Fettes on the spot, plied him with drinks, and honoured him with unusual confidences on his past career. If a tenth part of what he confessed were true, he was a very loathsome rogue; and the lad's vanity was tickled by the attention of so experienced a man.

'I'm a pretty bad fellow myself,' the stranger remarked, 'but Macfarlane is the boy—Toddy Macfarlane I call him. Toddy, order your friend another glass.' Or it might be, 'Toddy, you jump up and shut the door.' 'Toddy hates me,' he said again. 'Oh yes, Toddy, you do!'

'Don't you call me that confounded name,' growled Macfarlane.

'Hear him! Did you ever see the lads play knife? He would like to do that all over my body,' remarked the stranger.

'We medicals have a better way than that,' said Fettes. 'When we dislike a dead friend of ours, we dissect him.'

Macfarlane looked up sharply as though this jest were scarce to his mind.

The afternoon passed.   Gray, for that, was the stranger's name, invited Fettes to join them at dinner, ordered a feast so sumptuous that the tavern was thrown into commotion, and when all was done, commanded Macfarlane to settle the bill.   It was late before they separated; the man Gray was incapably drunk. Macfarlane, sobered by his fury, chewed the cud of the money he had been forced to squander and the slights he had been obliged to swallow.   Fettes, with various liquors singing in his head, returned home with devious footsteps and a mind entirely in abeyance.   The next day Macfarlane was absent from the class, and Fettes smiled to himself as he imagined him still squiring the intolerable Gray from tavern to tavern.   As soon as the hour of liberty had struck, he posted from place to place in quest of his last night's companions.   He could find them, however, nowhere; so he returned early to his rooms, went early to bed, and slept the sleep of the just.

At four in the morning, he was awakened by the well-known signal.   Descending to the door, he was filled with astonishment to find Macfarlane with his gig and, in the gig, one of those long and ghastly packages with which he was so well acquainted.

'What?' he cried.   'Have you been out alone?   How did you manage?'

But Macfarlane silenced him roughly, bidding him turn to business.   When they had got the body upstairs and laid it on the table, Macfarlane made at first as if he were going away.   Then he paused and seemed to hesitate, and then, 'You had better look at the face,' said he, in tones of some constraint.   'You had better,' he repeated, as Fettes only stared at him in wonder.

'But where, and how, and when did you come by it?' cried the other.

'Look at the face,' was the only answer.

Fettes was staggered; strange doubts assailed him. He looked from the young doctor to the body and then back again. At last, with a start, he did as he was bidden. He had almost expected the sight that met his eyes, and yet the shock was cruel. To see, fixed in the rigidity of death and naked on that coarse layer of sackcloth, the man whom he had left well-clad and full of meat and sin upon the threshold of a tavern, awoke, even in the thoughtless Fettes, some of the terrors of the conscience. It was a *cras tibi* which re-echoed in his soul that two whom he had known should have come to lie upon these icy tables. Yet these were only secondary thoughts. His first concern regarded Wolfe. Unprepared for a challenge so momentous, he knew not how to look his comrade in the face. He durst not meet his eye, and he had neither words nor voice at his command.

It was Macfarlane himself who made the first advance. He came up quietly behind and laid his hand gently but firmly on the other's shoulder.

'Richardson,' said he, 'may have the head.'

Now Richardson was a student who had long been anxious for that portion of the human subject to dissect. There was no answer, and the murderer resumed: 'Talking of business, you must pay me; your accounts, you see, must tally.'

Fettes found a voice, the ghost of his own: 'Pay you!' he cried. 'Pay you for that?'

'Why, yes, of course, you must. By all means and on every possible account, you must,' return the other. 'I dare not give it for nothing. You dare not take it for nothing; it would compromise us both. This is another case like Jane Galbraith's. The more things are wrong, the more we must act as if all were right.   Where does old K— keep his money?'

'There,' answered Fettes hoarsely, pointing to a cupboard in the corner.

'Give me the key, then,' said the other calmly, holding out his hand.

There was an instant's hesitation, and the die was cast. Macfarlane could not suppress a nervous twitch, the infinitesimal mark of immense relief, as he felt the key between his fingers. He opened the cupboard, brought out pen and ink and a paper book that stood in one compartment and separated from the funds in a drawer a sum suitable to the occasion.

'Now, look here,' he said, 'there is the payment made —first proof of your good faith: first step to your security. You have now to clinch it by a second. Enter the payment in your book, and then you for your part may defy the devil.'

The next few seconds were, for Fettes, an agony of thought, but in balancing his terrors, it was the most immediate that triumphed. Any future difficulty seemed almost welcome if he could avoid a present quarrel with Macfarlane. He set down the candle which he had been carrying all this time and with a steady hand, entered the date, the nature, and the amount of the transaction.

'And now,' said Macfarlane, 'it's only fair that you should pocket the lucre. I've had my share already. By the bye, when a man of the world falls into a bit of luck, has a few shillings extra in his pocket—I'm ashamed to speak of it, but there's a rule of conduct in the case. No treating, no purchase of expensive class-books, no squaring of old debts; borrow, don't lend.'

'Macfarlane,' began Fettes, still somewhat hoarsely, 'I have put my neck in a halter to oblige you.'

'To oblige me?' cried Wolfe. 'Oh, come! You did, as near as I can see the matter, what you downright had to do in self-defence. Suppose I got into trouble, where would you be? This second little matter flows clearly from the first. Mr Gray is the continuation of Miss Galbraith. You can't begin and then stop. If you begin, you must keep on beginning; that's the truth. No rest for the wicked.'

A horrible sense of blackness and the treachery of fate seized hold of the soul of the unhappy student.

'My God!' he cried, 'but what have I done? and when did I begin? To be made a class assistant—in the name of reason, where's the harm in that? Service wanted the position; Service might have got it. Would he have been where I am now?'

'My dear fellow,' said Macfarlane, 'what a boy you are! What harm has come to you? What harm can come to you if you hold your tongue? Why, man, do you know what this life is? There are two squads of us—the lions and the lambs. If you're a lamb, you'll come to lie upon these tables like Gray or Jane Galbraith; if you're a lion, you'll live and drive a horse like me, like K——, like all the world with any wit or courage. You're staggered at the first. But look at K——! My dear fellow, you're clever, you have pluck. I like you, and K—— likes you. You were born to lead the hunt, and I tell you, on my honour and my experience of life, three days from now, you'll laugh at all these scarecrows like a High School boy at a farce.'

And with that Macfarlane took his departure and drove off up the wynd in his gig to get under cover before daylight. Fettes was thus left alone with his regrets. He saw the miserable peril in which he stood involved. He saw, with inexpressible dismay, that there was no limit to his weakness and that, from concession to concession, he had fallen from the arbiter of Macfarlane's destiny to his paid and helpless accomplice. He would have given the world to have been a little braver at the time, but it did not occur to him that he might still be brave. The secret of Jane Galbraith and the cursed entry in the day book closed his mouth.

Hours passed; the class began to arrive; the members of the unhappy Gray were dealt out to one and to another and received without remark. Richardson was made happy with the head, and before the hour of freedom rang Fettes trembled with exultation to perceive how far they had already gone toward safety.

For two days. he continued to watch, with increasing joy, the dreadful process of disguise.

On the third day. Macfarlane made his appearance. He had been ill, he said; but he made up for lost time with the energy with which he directed the students. To Richardson, in particular, he extended the most valuable assistance and advice, and that student, encouraged by the praise of the demonstrator, burned high with ambitious hopes and saw the medal already in his grasp.

Before the week was out, Macfarlane's prophecy had been fulfilled. Fettes had outlived his terrors and had forgotten his baseness. He began to plume himself upon his courage and had so arranged the story in his mind that he could look back on these events with an unhealthy pride. Of his accomplice, he saw but little. They met, of course, in the business of the class; they received their orders together from Mr K—. At times they had a word or two in private, and Macfarlane was, from first to last, particularly kind and jovial. But it was plain that he avoided any reference to their common secret, and even when Fettes whispered to him that he had cast in his lot with the lions and foresworn the lambs, he only signed to him smilingly to hold his peace.

At length, an occasion arose that threw the pair once more into a closer union. Mr K— was again short of subjects; pupils were eager, and it was a part of this teacher's pretensions to be always well supplied. At the same time, there came the news of a burial in the rustic graveyard of Glencorse. Time has little changed the place in question. It stood then, as now, upon a cross road, out of the call of human habitations, and buried fathom deep in the foliage of six cedar trees. The cries of the sheep upon the neighbouring hills, the streamlets upon either hand, one loudly singing among pebbles, the other dripping furtively from pond to pond, the stir of the wind in mountainous old flowering chestnuts, and once in seven days the voice of the bell and the old tunes of the precentor, were the only sounds that disturbed the silence around the rural church. The Resurrection Man—to use a byname of the period—was not to be deterred by any of the sanctities of customary piety. It was part of his trade to despise and desecrate the scrolls and trumpets of old tombs, the paths worn by the feet of worshippers and mourners, and the offerings and the inscriptions of bereaved affection. To rustic neighbourhoods, where love is more than commonly tenacious and where some bonds of blood or fellowship unite the entire society of a parish, the body-snatcher, far from being repelled by natural respect, was attracted by the ease and safety of the task. To bodies that had been laid on the earth, in joyful expectation of a far different awakening, there came that hasty, lamp-lit, terror-haunted resurrection of the spade and mattock. The coffin was forced, the cerements torn, and the melancholy relics, clad in sackcloth, after being rattled for hours on moonless byways, were at length exposed to uttermost indignities before a class of gaping boys.

Somewhat as two vultures may swoop upon a dying lamb, Fettes and Macfarlane were to be let loose upon a grave in that green and quiet resting place. The wife of a farmer, a woman who had lived for sixty years, and been known for nothing but good butter and a godly conversation, was to be rooted from her grave at midnight and carried, dead and naked, to that far-away city that she had always honoured with her Sunday's best; the place beside her family was to be empty till the crack of doom; her innocent and almost venerable members to be exposed to that last curiosity of the anatomist.

Late one afternoon, the pair set forth, well-wrapped in cloaks and furnished with a formidable bottle. It rained without remission—a cold, dense, lashing rain. Now and again, there blew a puff of wind, but these sheets of falling water kept it down. Bottle and all, it was a sad and silent drive as far as Penicuik, where they were to spend the evening. They stopped once, to hide their implements in a thick bush not far from the churchyard, and once again at the Fisher's Tryst, to have a toast before the kitchen fire and vary their nips of whisky with a glass of ale. When they reached their journey's end, the gig was housed, the horse was fed and comforted, and the two young doctors in a private room sat down to the best dinner and the best wine the house afforded. The lights, the fire, the beating rain upon the window, and the cold, incongruous work that lay before them added zest to their enjoyment of the meal. With every glass, their cordiality increased. Soon Macfarlane handed a little pile of gold to his companion.

'A compliment,' he said. 'Between friends these little d-d accommodations ought to fly like pipe-lights.'

Fettes pocketed the money and applauded the sentiment to the echo. 'You are a philosopher,' he cried. 'I was an ass till I knew you. You and K— between you, by the Lord Harry! but you'll make a man of me.'

'Of course we shall,' applauded Macfarlane. 'A man? I tell you, it required a man to back me up the other morning. There are some big, brawling, forty-year-old cowards who would have turned sick at the look of the d—d thing; but not you—you kept your head. I watched you.'

'Well, and why not?' Fettes thus vaunted himself. 'It was no affair of mine. There was nothing to gain on the one side but disturbance, and on the other I could count on your gratitude, don't you see?' And he slapped his pocket till the gold pieces rang.

Macfarlane somehow felt a certain touch of alarm at these unpleasant words. He may have regretted that he had taught his young companion so successfully, but he had no time to interfere, for the other noisily continued in this boastful strain:—

'The great thing is not to be afraid. Now, between you and me, I don't want to hang—that's practical; but for all cant, Macfarlane, I was born with a contempt. Hell, God, Devil, right, wrong, sin, crime, and all the old gallery of curiosities—they may frighten boys, but men of the world, like you and me, despise them. Here's to the memory of Gray!'

It was by this time growing somewhat late. The gig, according to order, was brought round to the door with both lamps brightly shining, and the young men had to pay their bill and take the road. They announced that they were bound for Peebles and drove in that direction till they were clear of the last houses of the town; then, extinguishing the lamps, returned upon their course and followed a by-road toward Glencorse. There was no sound but that of their own passage and the incessant, strident pouring of the rain. It was pitch dark; here and there, a white gate or a white stone in the wall guided them for a short space across the night, but for the most part, it was at a foot pace and almost groping that they picked their way through that resonant blackness to their solemn and isolated destination. In the sunken woods that traverse the neighbourhood of the burying ground, the last glimmer failed them, and it became necessary to kindle a match and re-illumine one of the lanterns of the gig. Thus, under the dripping trees and environed by huge and moving shadows, they reached the scene of their unhallowed labours.

They were both experienced in such affairs, and powerful with the spade, and they had scarce been twenty minutes at their task before they were rewarded by a dull rattle on the coffin lid. At the same moment, Macfarlane, having hurt his hand upon a stone, flung it carelessly above his head. The grave, in which they now stood almost to the shoulders, was close to the edge of the plateau of the graveyard; and the gig lamp had been propped, the better to illuminate their labours, against a tree and on the immediate verge of the steep bank descending to the stream. Chance had taken a sure aim with the stone. Then came a clang of broken glass; night fell upon them; sounds alternately dull and ringing announced the bounding of the lantern down the bank and its occasional collision with the trees. A stone or two, which it had dislodged in its descent, rattled behind it into the profundities of the glen; and then silence, like night, resumed its sway; and they might bend their hearing to its utmost pitch, but naught was to be heard except the rain, now marching to the wind, now steadily falling over miles of open country.

They were so nearly at the end of their abhorred task that they judged it wisest to complete it in the dark. The coffin was exhumed and broken open; the body inserted in the dripping sack and carried between them to the gig; one mounted to keep it in its place, and the other, taking the horse by the mouth, groped along by wall and bush until they reached the wider road by the Fisher's Tryst. Here was a faint, diffused radiancy, which they hailed like daylight; by that, they pushed the horse to a good pace and began to rattle along merrily in the direction of the town.

They had both been wetted to the skin during their operations, and now, as the gig jumped among the deep ruts, the thing that stood propped between them fell now upon one and now upon the other. At every repetition of the horrid contact, each instinctively repelled it with greater haste, and the process, natural although it was, began to tell upon the nerves of the companions. Macfarlane made some ill-favoured jest about the farmer's wife, but it came hollowly from his lips and was allowed to drop in silence. Still, their unnatural burden bumped from side to side, and now the head would be laid, as if in confidence, upon their shoulders, and now the drenching sack-cloth would flap icily about their faces. A creeping chill began to possess the soul of Fettes. He peered at the bundle, and it seemed somehow larger than at first. All over the countryside and from every degree of distance, the farm dogs accompanied their passage with tragic ululations; and it grew and grew upon his mind that some unnatural miracle had been accomplished, that some nameless change had befallen the dead body, and that it was in fear of their unholy burden that the dogs were howling.

'For God's sake,' said he, making a great effort to arrive at speech, 'for God's sake, let's have a light!'

Seemingly Macfarlane was affected in the same direction; for, though he made no reply, he stopped the horse, passed the reins to his companion, got down, and proceeded to kindle the remaining lamp. They had by that time got no farther than the cross-road down to Auchenclinny. The rain still poured as though the deluge were returning, and it was no easy matter to make a light in such a world of wetness and darkness. When at last, the flickering blue flame had been transferred to the wick and began to expand and clarify and shed a wide circle of misty brightness around the gig, it became possible for the two young men to see each other and the thing they had along with them. The rain had moulded the rough sacking to the outlines of the body underneath; the head was distinct from the trunk, the shoulders plainly modelled; something at once spectral and human riveted their eyes upon the ghastly comrade of their drive.

For some time Macfarlane stood motionless, holding up the lamp. A nameless dread was swathed, like a wet sheet, about the body and tightened the white skin upon the face of Fettes; a fear that was meaningless, a horror of what could not be, kept mounting to his brain. Another beat of the watch, and he had spoken. But his comrade forestalled him.

'That is not a woman,' said Macfarlane in a hushed voice.

'It was a woman when we put her in,' whispered Fettes.

'Hold that lamp,' said the other. 'I must see her face.'

And as Fettes took the lamp, his companion untied the fastenings of the sack and drew down the cover from the head. The light fell very clear upon the dark, well-moulded features and smooth-shaven cheeks of a too-familiar countenance often beheld in dreams of both of these young men. A wild yell rang up into the night; each leapt from his own side into the roadway: the lamp fell, broke, and was extinguished; and the horse, terrified by this unusual commotion, bounded and went off toward Edinburgh at a gallop, bearing along with it, the sole occupant of the gig, the body of the dead and long-dissected Gray.

A GHOST STORY

by Mark Twain

I took a large room, far up Broadway, in a huge old building whose upper stories had been wholly unoccupied for years until I came. The place had long been given up to dust and cobwebs, solitude and silence. I seemed to grope among the tombs and invade the privacy of the dead that first night. I climbed up to my quarters. For the first time in my life, a superstitious dread came over me, and as I turned, a dark angle of the stairway and an invisible cobweb swung its sleazy woof in my face and clung there. I shuddered as one who had encountered a phantom.

I was glad enough when I reached my room and locked out the mold and the darkness. A cheery fire was burning in the grate, and I sat down before it with a comforting sense of relief. For two hours, I sat there, thinking of bygone times; recalling old scenes, and summoning half-forgotten faces out of the mists of the past; listening, in fancy, to voices that long ago grew silent for all time and to once familiar songs that nobody sings now. And as my reverie softened down to a sadder and sadder pathos, the shrieking of the winds outside softened to a wail, the angry beating of the rain against the panes diminished to a tranquil patter, and one by one, the noises in the street subsided, until the hurrying footsteps of the last belated straggler died away in the distance and left no sound behind.

The fire had burned low. A sense of loneliness crept over me. I arose and undressed, moving on tiptoe about the room, doing stealthily what I had to do as if I were environed by sleeping enemies whose slumbers it would be fatal to break. I covered up in bed and lay listening to the rain and wind and the faint creaking of distant shutters till they lulled me to sleep.

I slept profoundly, but for how long, I do not know. All at once, I found myself awake and filled with a shuddering expectancy. All was still. All but my own heart —I could hear it beat. Presently the bedclothes began to slip away slowly toward the foot of the bed as if someone were pulling them! I could not stir; I could not speak. Still, the blankets slipped deliberately away till my breast was uncovered. Then with a great effort, I seized them and drew them over my head. I waited, listened, waited. Once more, that steady pull began, and once more, I lay torpid for a century of dragging seconds till my breast was naked again. At last, I roused my energies and snatched the covers back to their place, and held them with a strong grip. I waited. By and by, I felt a faint tug and took a fresh grip. The tug strengthened to a steady strain—it grew stronger and stronger. My hold parted, and for the third time, the blankets slid away. I groaned. An answering groan came from the foot of the bed! Beaded drops of sweat stood on my forehead. I was dead than alive. Presently I heard a heavy footstep in my room—the step of an elephant, it seemed to me—it was not like anything human. But it was moving from me—there was relief in that. I heard it approach the door—pass out without moving bolt or lock—and wander away among the dismal corridors, straining the floors and joists till they creaked again as it passed—and then silence reigned once more.

When my excitement had calmed, I said to myself, "This is a dream—simply a hideous dream." And so I lay thinking it over until I convinced myself that it was a dream, and then a comforting laugh relaxed my lips, and I was happy again. I got up and struck a light, and when I found that the locks and bolts were just as I had left them, another soothing laugh welled in my heart and rippled from my lips. I took my pipe and lit it and was just sitting down before the fire when—down went the pipe out of my nerveless fingers, the blood forsook my cheeks, and my placid breathing was cut short with a gasp! In the ashes on the hearth, side by side with my own bare footprint, was another, so vast that in comparison, mine was but an infant's! Then I had a visitor, and the elephant tread was explained.

I put out the light and returned to bed, palsied with fear. I lay a long time, peering into the darkness and listening.—Then I heard a grating noise overhead, like the dragging of a heavy body across the floor, then the throwing down of the body, and the shaking of my windows in response to the concussion. In distant parts of the building, I heard the muffled slamming of doors. I heard, at intervals, stealthy footsteps creeping in and out among the corridors and up and down the stairs.

Sometimes these noises approached my door, hesitated, and went away again. I heard the clanking of chains faintly in remote passages and listened while the clanking grew nearer—while it wearily climbed the stairways, marking each move by the loose surplus of chain that fell with an accented rattle upon each succeeding step as the goblin that bore it advanced. I heard muttered sentences; half-uttered screams that seemed smothered violently; and the swish of invisible garments, the rush of invisible wings. Then I became conscious that my chamber was invaded—that I was not alone. I heard sighs and breathings about my bed and mysterious whisperings. Three little spheres of soft phosphorescent light appeared on the ceiling directly over my head, clung and glowed there a moment, and then dropped—two of them upon my face and one upon the pillow. They spattered, liquidly, and felt warm. Intuition told me they had turned to gouts of blood as they fell—I needed no light to satisfy myself of that. Then I saw pallid faces, dimly luminous, and white uplifted hands, floating bodiless in the air—floating a moment and then disappearing. The whispering ceased, and the voices and the sounds and a solemn stillness followed. I waited and listened. I felt that I must have light or die. I was weak with fear. I slowly raised myself toward a sitting posture, and my face came in contact with a clammy hand! All strength went from me, apparently, and I fell back like a stricken invalid. Then I heard the rustle of a garment—it seemed to pass to the door and go out.

When everything was still once more, I crept out of bed, sick and feeble, and lit the gas with a hand that trembled as if it were aged with a hundred years. The light brought some little cheer to my spirits. I sat down and fell into a dreamy contemplation of that great footprint in the ashes. By and by, its outlines began to waver and grow dim. I glanced up, and the broad gas flame was slowly wilting away. At the same moment, I heard that elephantine tread again. I noted its approach, nearer and nearer, along the musty halls, and dimmer and dimmer the light waned. The tread reached my very door and paused —the light had dwindled to a sickly blue, and all things about me lay in a spectral twilight. The door did not open, and yet I felt a faint gust of air fan my cheek and presently was conscious of a huge, cloudy presence before me. I watched it with fascinated eyes. A pale glow stole over the Thing; gradually, its cloudy folds took shape—an arm appeared, then legs, then a body, and last, a great sad face looked out of the vapor. Stripped of its filmy housings, naked, muscular and comely, the majestic Cardiff Giant loomed above me!

All my misery vanished—for a child might know that no harm could come with that benignant countenance. My cheerful spirits returned at once, and in sympathy, with them, the gas flamed up brightly again. Never a lonely outcast was so glad to welcome company as I was to greet the friendly giant. I said:

"Why, is it nobody but you? Do you know, I have been scared to death for the last two or three hours? I am most honestly glad to see you. I wish I had a chair—Here, here, don't try to sit down in that thing—"

But it was too late. He was in it before I could stop him, and down he went—I never saw a chair shiver so in my life.

"Stop, stop, you'll ruin ev—"

Too late again. There was another crash, and another chair was resolved into its original elements.

"Confound it. Haven't you got any judgment at all? Do you want to ruin all the furniture in the place? Here, here, you petrified fool—"

But it was no use. Before I could arrest him, he had sat down on the bed, and it was a melancholy ruin.

"Now, what sort of a way is that to do? First, you come lumbering about the place bringing a legion of vagabond goblins along with you to worry me to death, and then when I overlook an indelicacy of costume which would not be tolerated anywhere by cultivated people except in a respectable theater and not even there if the nudity were of your sex, you repay me by wrecking all the furniture you can find to sit down on. And why will you? You damage yourself as much as you do me. You have broken off the end of your spinal column and littered up the floor with chips of your hams till the place looks like a marble yard. You ought to be ashamed of yourself—you are big enough to know better."

"Well, I will not break any more furniture. But what am I to do? I have not had a chance to sit down for a century." And the tears came into his eyes.

"Poor devil," I said, "I should not have been so harsh with you. And you are an orphan, too, no doubt. But sit down on the floor here—nothing else can stand your weight—and besides, we cannot be sociable with you away up there above me; I want you down where I can perch on this high counting-house stool and gossip with you face to face."

So he sat down on the floor, and lit a pipe which I gave him, threw one of my red blankets over his shoulders, inverted my sitz-bath on his head, helmet fashion, and made himself picturesque and comfortable. Then he crossed his ankles, while I renewed the fire and exposed the flat, honeycombed bottoms of his prodigious feet to the grateful warmth.

"What is the matter with the bottom of your feet and the back of your legs, that they are gouged up so?"

"Infernal chilblains—I caught them clear up to the back of my head, roosting out there under Newell's farm. But I love the place; I love it as one loves his old home. There is no peace for me like the peace I feel when I am there."

We talked along for half an hour, and then I noticed that he looked tired and spoke of it.

"Tired?" he said. "Well, I should think so. And now I will tell you all about it, since you have treated me so well. I am the spirit of the Petrified Man that lies across the street there in the museum. I am the ghost of the Cardiff Giant. I can have no rest, no peace, till they have given that poor body burial again. Now what was the most natural thing for me to do to make men satisfy this wish? Terrify them into it!— haunt the place where the body lay! So I haunted the museum night after night. I even got other spirits to help me. But it did no good, for nobody ever came to the museum at midnight. Then it occurred to me to come over the way and haunt this place a little. I felt that if I ever got a hearing I must succeed, for I had the most efficient company that perdition could furnish. Night after night we have shivered around through these mildewed halls, dragging chains, groaning, whispering, tramping up and down stairs, till, to tell you the truth, I am almost worn out. But when I saw a light in your room to-night I roused my energies again and went at it with a deal of the old freshness. But I am tired out—entirely fagged out. Give me, I beseech you, give me some hope!"

I lit off my perch in a burst of excitement and exclaimed:

"This transcends everything! everything that ever did occur! Why you poor blundering old fossil, you have had all your trouble for nothing—you have been haunting a plaster cast of yourself—the real Cardiff Giant is in Albany! —[A fact. The original fraud was ingeniously and fraudfully duplicated, and exhibited in New York as the "only genuine" Cardiff Giant (to the unspeakable disgust of the owners of the real colossus) at the very same time that the latter was drawing crowds at a museum in Albany,]—Confound it, don't you know your own remains?"

I never saw such an eloquent look of shame, of pitiable humiliation, overspread a countenance before.

The Petrified Man rose slowly to his feet and said:

"Honestly, is that true?"

"As true as I am sitting here."

He took the pipe from his mouth and laid it on the mantel, then stood irresolute a moment (unconsciously, from old habit, thrusting his hands where his pantaloons pockets should have been and meditatively dropping his chin on his breast) and finally said:

"Well—I never felt so absurd before. The Petrified Man has sold everybody else, and now the mean fraud has ended by selling its own ghost! My son, if there is any charity left in your heart for a poor friendless phantom like me, don't let this get out. Think how you would feel if you had made such an ass of yourself."

I heard his stately tramp die away, step by step, down the stairs and out into the deserted street, and felt sorry that he was gone, poor fellow—and sorrier still that he had carried off my red blanket and my bathtub.

A Final Farewell

We have journeyed together through shadowed corridors and haunted halls, our hearts pounding in unison with the rhythm of each chilling tale. From the first flicker of fear in Volume One to the deepening shadows of Volume Two, you have been our constant companion.

Your courage in facing the unknown, your imagination ignited by the macabre, and your unwavering support have been the lifeblood of this eerie endeavour. We hope that these stories have not only entertained but also provoked thought, challenged perceptions, and perhaps even stirred a touch of the supernatural within you.

As we bid adieu for now, remember that the world of the uncanny is vast and ever-present. Shadows dance in the corners of your mind, and whispers of the unseen may linger in the quiet moments. Keep your senses sharp, your imagination alive, and your courage unwavering.

Until our paths cross again in the realm of the unknown, may your nights be filled with sweet dreams (or perhaps, delightfully disturbing ones).

Thank you for sharing this chilling adventure.